THE CAPE MURDERS

THE CAPE MURDERS

Dolores Weeks

DODD, MEAD & COMPANY
New York

The characters and situations in this book are entirely fictitious
and bear no relationship to any real person or actual event.

Published by Dodd, Mead & Company, Inc.,
71 Fifth Avenue, New York, N.Y. 10003
Manufactured in the United States of America
Production supervision by Mike Cantalupo
First Edition

1 2 3 4 5 6 7 8 9 10

Library of Congress Cataloging-in-Publication Data

Weeks, Dolores.
     The cape murders.

     I. Title.
PS3573. E325C3   1987   813'.54   87-19924
ISBN 0-396-09102-4

For Allen

With Special Thanks to
Zola Helen Ross

One

Dr. Scott Eason was on the deck of his summer cabin, soaking up the morning sun and trying hard not to think about the surgical practice he'd walked away from in Seattle, when Al Turner burst in, his bony chest rising and falling in great gulps. Al was a retired professor of ancient history and in pretty good shape for a man in his mid-seventies, but right now he looked like an out-of-breath scarecrow.

"Come . . . quick . . . Scottie. S-somebody shot Owen . . . Went . . . worth."

It was, of course, exactly the sort of thing Scott was trying to avoid. The trouble was, Al looked desperate. Scott squeezed into his tennis shoes and slipped on a shirt. "Did you run all the way?"

Al nodded, not wasting his breath on an answer.

"Dumb thing to do!" The old man could easily have a coronary running in the heat, and a dozen Owen Wentworths weren't worth one Al Turner.

Scott snatched the key to the Jeep from the kitchen table and started for the door. The large black and white sheep dog that had been lying beside him on the deck rose to follow. "Not this time, Dandy."

It was a little under a mile, over dirt and rock roads, to Owen's cabin. There were strict rules on the island about driving speeds in the dust season. Scott broke them all. "How bad is it?" he asked as they bumped along, stirring up a thick cloud behind them.

Al set his thin lips in a grimace and shook his head. "Don't know," he said, getting his wind back slowly. "Millie ran out of Owen's place . . . said to get you quick. You know Millie—takes a lot to unnerve her."

It was a strong indication of trouble, Scott agreed, and he pressed his foot harder on the accelerator. Scott could think of a dozen people in Seattle who might enjoy inflicting bodily harm on the high-living attorney, but this wasn't Seattle. This was a quiet summer community on Cape San Juan.

Owen's house stood in a small stand of wind-shorn firs, isolated from its nearest neighbor by a hundred feet of sand, grass, and brush. It was a flat-topped rambler, fair in size for the Cape, with a wide deck that hung over the rocks, the beach ten feet below. Large picture windows and skylight bubbles everywhere made it look like a plastic box.

Scott and the professor piled out of the Jeep and raced toward the house. Millie Rogers poked her gray head from around the breezeway.

"In there," she said in a high-pitched quivering voice as she pointed to the door. She was ghostly pale and shivering, even though the temperature was already in the seventies. Millie was the day woman from Friday Harbor who cleaned for most of the summer people on the Cape. She'd been widowed for ten years, raised her teenage daughter herself, and was what Scott thought of as levelheaded. The front door was standing wide open. Scott and Al walked through ahead of her.

The inside reeked of whiskey and tobacco, not an uncommon condition for Owen's place. They found the attorney in the living room, lying in the middle of the big ivory area carpet, his blood spilled all over it.

Al drew in his breath. "Oh, my God!"

Owen was a big man, inclined to overweight and tall, at least three inches taller than Scott, who stood right at six feet. Owen had been good-looking once, but in the last few years dissipation had brought on heavy jowls and puffiness under the eyes. At forty-four, he looked sixty.

Right now, Owen, dressed in a brightly flowered sports shirt and jeans, lay out flat on his back, his big head resting on the carpet and his long legs stretched over the carpet fringe onto the oak-planked floor. His mouth was open, and he was staring straight up into one of his skylights. The sun shone down on his stomach. It was ripped open so he looked like one of the rabbits run over on the Cape road. In the ten years Scott had been in surgical practice, he'd developed a necessary objectivity about death and violence, but as he looked at Owen with a hole in his abdomen the size of a baseball, he thought he'd never really get used to it. "Oh, hell!" He sighed.

He pressed a finger to the attorney's neck. No pulse. He pulled back on the eyelid. No corneal reflex. He'd been dead for some time.

Scott shook his head at the professor. "A job for the coroner, I'm afraid."

The old man didn't say a word. He held on to a chair, his small blue eyes glazed over. He looked as if he might be sick.

"Better sit down, Al."

The professor folded up into the chair. "Shotgun?"

Scott nodded. "The only thing I know of that could drive a hole like that. Did anyone call the police?"

"I did," Millie said, picking her way around the potted palm tree, keeping her distance from Owen. She'd come from town that morning to clean for Owen after his party of the night before. "I found him just like that." She tossed her head in Owen's general direction, not looking at him. "Didn't feel I should leave till you came. Must've lost my head. It was the sight of all that blood, and those eyes, staring at nothing. I called Leroy. That was twenty minutes ago. Can't imagine what's keeping him. He was only coming from Friday Harbor. Doesn't take that long, the way *he* drives. I would've cleaned up this mess, but Leroy said I wasn't to touch a thing." She stared at the room sorrowfully.

Scott laid an arm around the slender shoulders and gave her a squeeze. "You did fine, Millie." He signaled the professor with his eyes, but the old man wasn't looking too good himself and didn't pick up on it. "Al, why don't you take Millie outside to get some air."

"Be happy to," Al said, and, taking Millie by the arm, steered her to the door.

Alone, Scott surveyed the rooms in which Owen had breathed his last. The house said much about the attorney—contemporary, almost everything white, the walls, sectional sofa and chairs, the rug. Even the tables were of glass and blond wood. The only exceptions were the African artifacts displayed throughout the rooms. Owen had been into African art in a big way—carved figures into ebony and ivory, wood ritual objects, masks and headpieces—but his obsession clearly had been death masks. A row of them hung down the hall like inverted clown faces in blacks, whites, and browns. He used to boast he paid a half-million dollars for his collection, surprising because he'd always been such a sharp operator, and African art was a high-risk business.

The house wasn't designed for privacy. Someone standing in the middle of the living room could see directly into the master suite and study. Rumor had it Owen wandered in the nude, giving passing boaters an eyeful, and there were ugly stories about his overnight guests and perversions.

Scott strolled down the marble-tiled hall and looked into the bedroom. Everything in place. Beds not slept in. The kitchen was a different story. Three empty fifths of Gordon's gin, two large empty bottles of Seagram's, and a half-empty bottle of Ballentyne's stood on the counter that divided the kitchen from the living area. The ice buckets were full of water, and a tray of leftover shrimp and crabs' legs were starting to smell up the dining room. The ashtrays spilled cigarette butts onto the floor, and unwashed highball glasses were putting rings on the tables.

Al returned and stood tentatively in the entryway. "I left Millie on the beach. She'll be all right. Sea air was just what she needed."

They heard the siren first, then tires braking on gravel. A car door slammed. Al grinned. "Big Buck has arrived."

Leroy Freeman walked in with his usual air of self-importance. The Colt .38 was strapped to his side and the Stetson firmly planted on his head. He took one look at Owen. "Dead?"

Scott nodded. "I'd say four or five hours."

"I better call Frank."

Leroy strode into the kitchen, barked orders over the phone to the mortician in Friday Harbor. "It's going to run in the eighties today, so get a move on." It was the only indication the sheriff was upset. He studied Owen a moment, then glanced out the window. "Tide's changing." He removed his hat and mopped the brown strands of hair that matted around his temples, exposing a thin line of pale skin on his otherwise darkly tanned face. "Hot in here." He dropped the hat on the sofa and faced Scott. "Shotgun!"

Scott nodded. "Fired at close range. Pushed pieces of his pants into the abdominal cavity."

"Anything else?"

"Struck an artery, ruptured the spleen. Died in five, ten minutes."

"Painful?"

"Damn."

Leroy walked around the room, took in the mess. "Quite a party. You one of the guests?"

"No."

Leroy turned to the professor.

"Don't look at me," Al snapped. "I was *not* a friend of Owen Wentworth."

"Where's Millie?"

"Outside."

"Call her in, would you?"

Scott and Al exchanged glances.

"Don't you want to cover him up first, Sheriff?" Al said.

"Oh, hell." Leroy stalked down the hall to the bedroom

5

wing and started opening doors. He rummaged through the linen closet until he found a sheet, pulled it out, and draped it over the body so only Owen's sandaled feet stuck out the end. "Now, do you suppose we can get Millie in here?"

Millie's eyes went right to the spot. She relaxed when she saw the sheet. Yes, she said, she had a key to the house. Had keys to most of the houses on the Cape, since very often she cleaned after the summer people left for the mainland. As a general rule, she liked to air the places between cleanings. "Houses closed up get musty. A little sea breeze does wonders for sweetening the air. Owen's was the worst for bad air. Cigar smoke. Enough to make a person sick. Real bad this morning. My sinuses started acting up soon as I opened the door. Don't know how I'll ever get the blood off that rug. Never could keep it clean. Always getting liquor spilled on it. Whole house is like that. A mess after one of his weekends."

"He entertained a lot?"

A smile tugged at Millie's lips. "Long as I been cleaning for the man—going on six years next month—it's been one party after another."

"Ever been to one of these parties?"

"Sometimes I served if he was having a sit-down dinner."

"And last night?"

"That was one of his drinking affairs."

"Who came?"

"I wouldn't know. I never went to those."

"Not any of them?"

"No."

"What about the dinner parties?"

"I never thought it my business to keep a list."

Leroy tried pinning her down, but Millie had a code, and no amount of persuading swayed her.

"So all of the Cape and half the island could've been on his guest list?" Leroy said in an irritated voice.

"It's possible."

Leroy threw Millie a disgusted look and went back to

questioning the professor. Al repeated what he'd told Scott. He was on his usual morning stroll, returning from American Camp, about nine-thirty, when he ran into Millie on the road. She told him to get the doctor, that Owen had been shot. He didn't stop to ask questions. He just rushed right over to get Scott.

Leroy whipped out a notepad from his back pocket and began writing. "You passed the house twice?"

"That's right."

"What time was it on your first pass?"

Al thought a moment. "Eight, or thereabouts."

"Takes you that long to walk from American Camp?"

"I stopped at the digs."

"Did you see anything different when you were walking?"

"Mmm. Saw the big bald eagle circle over the lighthouse. A small doe sprang out of that grove of Norwegian pine on Chapman's drive."

Leroy sighed impatiently. "*Hear* anything?"

"Heard the gill-netters going back from Eagle Cove. Sherman's roosters were crowing. Heard the jets taking off from McCord."

"Hear anything like a shot?"

"No, but I don't think I would with the noise of the big diesels. And those jets sound like a bolt of thunder sometimes. Hard to hear anything over that."

Leroy wrote it all down. "Anybody touch anything here?"

"No."

Leroy paused in front of one of the death masks. It was particularly hideous, with a ropelike braid that dangled along the pointed jaw to the chin. Perversely, it brought to Scott's mind a hanging.

"Tell me, Doc, what the hell are these things?"

Scott smiled. "African art. Mid–seventeenth century, I think. Some of them represent religious rituals, fertility rites, ceremonial stuff. That one is a death mask."

"Expensive?"

"Very."

He shook his head in bewilderment, and Scott felt an instant bond with Leroy.

"How well did you know Wentworth, Doc?"

"About like everyone on the Cape. None of us *really* knew him."

"Why's that? From the looks of things here, he was a very friendly fellow."

"Outwardly, he was affable enough."

"What in hell does *that* mean?"

The professor sniffed impatiently. "What Scottie's trying to tell you is the man was one of those hail-and-well-met boys, who, given half a chance, would pick your pockets and start on your mother-in-law's gold inlays."

"Do you speak from personal knowledge, Professor Turner?" Leroy asked.

"I do not."

"That include you, Doc?"

"No."

Leroy had a tendency to repeat himself. He went over their stories again. "And this morning while you were sunbathing, Doctor, did *you* hear or see anything?"

"No, but I'm quite a distance. I don't think I would."

"Sound carries on the water, particularly a gunshot."

Certainly Scott's neighbors had complained often enough about the music that blared from Owen's stereo on clear nights. Scott didn't say anything.

"What about his next-door neighbors?"

"Fred and Lorene Chapman. They're off the island right now."

"How do you know that?"

"They're friends of mine. I saw them off last Friday."

"How can I get hold of them?"

"You could call Fred at his office in Seattle. He's with Price and Sloan, stockbrokers. I don't think he can help much. He and his wife weren't friendly with Owen."

"Who was?"

8

Al answered. "A few people around here would go anywhere for a free drink, but Owen was not well loved."

Leroy said he'd check out Fred's cottage for a break-in, just in case this was a simple burglary, although nothing in the condition of the house lent itself to this theory. Scott and Al left.

Al was quiet on the drive back. The sun burned bright overhead. Along the sandy shoulders of the road the pine trees were parched gray, almost black, like the death masks, like Owen's face. Scott knew he ought to feel remorse, but couldn't.

As if reading his mind, the professor said, "Only the good die young. Owen must've been a lot older than I thought."

"Did you know he was throwing a party last night?"

"Didn't even know he was on the island. He usually doesn't roll in until Friday night. This is Thursday, remember?"

"Didn't see him yesterday on your walk?"

"No, but that's not unusual. He always slept till noon."

Scott pulled up in front of the professor's cabin. "I didn't know you walked as far as American Camp every day, Al."

"Anything wrong with that?" The old man's testiness was a sure sign he was still upset.

"No. You have more energy than I, that's all."

"That's nothing to be proud of. Here you are—big strapping fellow—only thirty-five."

"Thirty-seven."

The old man sniffed and said nothing.

"How about dinner?"

The suggestion warmed him up, and he nodded agreement. "But you'll have to come here. I'm not sticking my big toe out tonight."

Scott nodded agreeably. "I'll bring the steaks. How's seven suit you?"

"Suits me fine."

When Scott wheeled the Jeep onto his drive, the sheriff was waiting. Leroy stepped out of the patrol car, wearing a catty expression, and Scott guessed he'd discovered something about Owen's murder. He was holding a small piece of glossy paper, worn on the edges. He handed it to Scott. "I think this belongs to you."

Scott looked at the photograph of a woman's face, and a lump settled painfully in his throat. It was Toni, raven hair, flashing brown eyes, as beautiful and vibrant as the day they'd married. Scott felt the force of Leroy's gaze. He hoped the moisture starting at the corners of his eyes didn't show. "Where?" he said, fighting to keep his voice even. "Where did you get this?"

"Didn't I tell you? I found it in Owen Wentworth's wallet."

Two

The thought of Toni and Owen brought an ache to Scott's chest. He couldn't believe it. Yet, looking back over the last year, it fit in many ways—her drinking, running up to their cabin by herself when she professed to hate the island, swings in her moods, not her normal pattern at all. And there'd been someone. He'd known that.

Leroy's voice came from a great distance. "Any reason your wife's picture would turn up in Owen's wallet?"

Scott shook his head in bewilderment. "We were separated before . . . before—" Scott cleared his throat and tried again. "Before her death," he finished softly.

Leroy kicked at a rock. "I heard about the accident. I don't like asking this, Doc, but was there anything between her and Wentworth?"

Scott shook his head at Leroy and thought to himself, But I don't know. I don't really know.

"Did your wife go to Wentworth's parties?"

"We went to a few, years ago."

"Why did you stop?"

"I've never been much for that kind of thing."

"What about your wife?"

"She didn't mind them."

"You ever do business with Wentworth?"

"No."

"Why not?"

"I have my own attorney in Seattle."

Leroy looked off at the water and then down at his shoelaces. "How long ago was the accident?"

"Six months next Sunday." And they'd lost the baby eight months before that. He'd never forget the despairing look in her eyes when they told her she couldn't have another.

Leroy's voice broke in again. "You say you were separated. When was that?"

"A month before the accident." Scott stirred. "Leroy, I don't see the point in all of this."

Leroy removed his hat and mopped his head. His big face was sympathetic. "Sorry, Doc, it's my job to ask questions. Doesn't mean I have to like it." He started for his car. "Say, on those African masks. Did you notice one was missing?"

Puzzled, Scott shook his head. "No, can't say I did."

"Gone, all right. Left a mark on the bedroom wall. Oh, I checked out the neighbors' house. Everything looks okay." He paused by his car door. "Maybe I can get you to fill me in on those African artifacts one of these days."

"Be glad to do what I can," Scott said, sighing, "but my wife was the authority on the subject."

Long after Leroy left, Scott stood on the deck staring blankly at the water, thinking of Toni and trying to imagine her with Owen. Six years living with someone, you'd think you'd know those things, which only showed how far apart they'd actually been. Toni had lived in her own private world of high fashions, New York buying trips, shows, meetings. She found island life too slow. That first time he'd brought her to the Cape, she spent the entire weekend studying the winter lines for the store and never set foot on the beach. When he asked her to sail in the *Picaroon*, a terrified look came over her face, and she shook her head fiercely.

"I hate the water," she said.

No wonder. She couldn't swim a stroke.

A gull landed on the long piece of driftwood below the rocks. Scott grabbed the binoculars from the kitchen table and found a spot on the south corner of the deck where the sun beat down the strongest. He stretched out on the webbed chaise, one of a pair of bright yellow folding lounges Toni had bought for his birthday two years before. For a moment he imagined her snuggled up beside him, her toe poking against the calf of his leg. He reached out to touch her, and his hand fell on Dandy's long fur. Scott jerked up, and sweat trickled down the back of his neck. The gull flew off the log, soared overhead, and landed on the kelp.

There had to be a reasonable explanation for Toni's picture in Owen's wallet, one that didn't leave this taste of bitterness. Toni and Owen. Like the way she'd died, there was something very wrong about it.

Then it struck him. Does Leroy think I killed Owen? Leroy could be maddeningly noncommunicative at times, but he was no fool. Still, someone murdered Owen. Leroy couldn't rule out anyone. Fortunately for Fred and Lorene, they'd picked this week to go off island. If they'd been there last night they might have heard those shots, might have stumbled over Owen's killer.

Scott considered calling Fred with the bad news—or good, depending on how one looked at it—and quickly rejected the idea. They'd find out soon enough, and to be honest about it, he had no desire to do anything that might hasten their return to the island. It had only been a week since they'd left, a week without Lorene's intrusions. Scott had been there to see them off.

"C'mon, Lorene," Fred had said. "It's two-thirty, and I need to be in that meeting at four."

"It takes an hour and a half to get to Shishole," Scott said in disbelief.

Fred grinned and held up one finger.

"One hour? You must be running on jet fuel."

"He always travels like that," Lorene said, laughing as she trudged up behind them, a strand of ash-blond hair in the way of one eye. Lorene was a big-boned woman, but she was puffing under the strain of the load she was carrying. Fred, slightly built and two inches shorter than his wife, took her physical capacities for granted.

Scott relieved Lorene of the pile, loaded it into the Bayliner, and helped undo the lines. He waved at the two of them as they backed out of the slip. Lorene was talking all the way.

"Call Cynthia."

Scott pretended not to hear. Lorene had been pushing Cynthia Woods at him for weeks, and though Scott had nothing against Lorene's friend, liked her, actually, he resented being matched up.

"I mean it, Scottie. She's expecting you to call."

Fred played the innocent. "You have the keys to the Mercedes. Go ahead and use it."

"No, thanks."

"We'll be back as soon as I get things squared away," Fred said and added something else that died in the roar of his big outboard.

The small boat took off like one of the jet foils and planed across the water at high speed. An hour to Seattle? Scott shook his head. For a sane man, at least two. He'd cautioned Fred about it once. "Those waters can get damn rough."

"Yeah," Fred said with the lopsided grin, "but I move quick."

"What if your engine conks out? Do you have an auxiliary?"

"Nope," Fred replied breezily, appraising his nineteen-foot Bayliner with obvious pride. "If the engine goes, I've had it."

Lorene laughed at Scott's frown. "That's just Fred, Scottie. You should know that."

How wonderful it must be to hold such an easygoing outlook on life.

The water clicked peacefully across the rocks. From behind the driftwood below the deck, there was a flapping of giant wings as a great bald eagle took off from a log. In flight he caught an air current and slowly circled the swirling waters in front of the deck.

Scott regarded this corner of the islands as a world apart, one that he needed right now. Yet few of his friends understood. Certainly not his partner, Ralph Nelson. When Scott told Ralph he was quitting practice to move full-time to the island, Ralph typically leaped to his own conclusions.

"I don't like to speak ill of the dead, but Toni was never right for you. Look on the positive side. You've no children, no alimony. You'll meet someone else." Twice divorced, Ralph had views that reflected his own outlook on marriage. "You're no Greek god, but you have that rugged look some women fancy."

He wasn't a pretty man, wouldn't have liked it much if he were. An average face, he supposed. He ran his hands through his hair. Hair and eyebrows bleached from the sun, a bit too much, perhaps. He was healthy-looking, anyway.

"At least blonds don't show gray," Ralph said.

"I'm not gray, Ralph."

"The point is you're too old to go running around barefoot like a beach bum."

"That's not the idea." Scott tried to explain Toni wasn't the reason he was quitting. He and Ralph had been over it a thousand times, how medicine had become a computerized paper factory where the patient-doctor relationship was losing to HMOs, rules, and malpractice suits. Everyone questioned. No one trusted. The patient had lost the right to choose. The doctor had lost his independence of judgment. No, he'd had his fill. Without Toni to consider, the decision had been easy.

"How are you going to get along without an income? Had you thought about that?"

"I may go back to commercial fishing. That's how I paid my way through med school."

Ralph smiled. "You'll be back by the end of the summer, when you've worked this out of your system."

Ralph never had been a good listener.

Scott set the binoculars on the deck, stretched out under the sun, and closed his eyes. Toni was dead, so was Owen, and life went on.

He woke to Dandy's wet nose nuzzling his feet. A slight breeze had started up, and he wondered how long he'd slept. Out on the water a new procession of small boats strained against the powerful current. The flood tide was well under way. The passage, which had been as calm as a stagnant pool earlier, now turned and foamed like a river after the spring thaw.

Eventually, the boat traffic thinned, and there was only the small blue silhouettes of the giant tankers in the distance, heading east to Anacortes to unload the oil from Alaska's north slopes.

Laughter trailed up from the beach. The cocktail hour had begun for his neighbors. Someone shouted, "Bring the steaks," and there was more laughter. All at once, Scott felt an urge, a deep longing to be part of it. From the rock ledge between their properties, Paul Martin waved. Scott waved back, and the feeling passed. He was the third man now, and conversation had a discouraging way of ending up in a discussion of Toni or his views on medicine, all of which required painful explanation. Maybe Ralph was right. He was a natural-born recluse.

The shadows on the water lengthened and the pass turned into a pond again as the flood tide was complete. On the strait a hazy mist began to settle over Partridge Point, and Scott wondered if it were going to bring in the fog. From the distance he heard the deep chugging of a diesel. Three masts appeared over Goose Island's hump. Scott perked up. "Gotta be a big one."

He stationed himself on the corner of the deck so as to spot her as she rounded the island. In a few seconds the rest of her came into view. A staysail schooner, gaff-rigged, fore and aft, with a flying forsail. He held his binoculars on her. Beautiful! Didn't see many like her anymore. Eighty feet, if she were an inch.

The sails were up and hanging limp as she moved under power. Her long sheer cabin hugged the decks. An aftercabin sat gracefully behind the wheelhouse, and two dinghies hung from her davits behind the mizzenmast. Quite a contrast to his own little sloop. This ship could stack three or four *Picaroons* alongside and still have room to spare. He tried to make out her name, but there was nothing on her forward gunwale, no name, no numbers. She flew Canadian colors. Had to be a ship of registry. Funny he hadn't seen her before. He held the glasses on her, admired the sleekness of lines as she motored into the channel. Something else different. The gaff-rigging. Always gave them the look of a pirate ship.

A camp following of gulls and terns, mostly terns, trailed

the ship. Smaller in size and swifter than the gulls, the grayish seabirds put on a spectacular show. Squeals of *kik-kik-kik* filled the air as they flew straight up, tucked neatly, and plunged straight down, zipping into the water like bullets.

Another flicker of light, steel flashing. Movement on the afterdeck. Three men worked around the jigger halyards. Scott ran the glasses on them. One was tall and wore a yellow slicker. Another was short, built like an ape with long arms. He wore a stocking knit cap and a heavy sweater. The third was tall, bone-skinny, lightly dressed in jeans and bare to the waist. The movements of these men, strained and jerky, contrasted sharply with the graceful sweep of the birds.

The terns worked the water near the kelp bed. One by one they struck the water like bright-silver knives. On the schooner's stern an arm went up, and metal glistened, almost like one of the terns. A splash off the starboard kicked up a fountain of spray. Water spurted and died in a circular puddle of foam.

The helmsman was forward of the mizzenmast, nearly hidden by a half-dozen cylinders of deck cargo. Aft of the cabin, two crewmen, one short with long arms, the other wiry and tall, secured the lines around the cleats. No yellow slicker was visible. Scott ran the glasses over the ship, looking for the third man. No sign of him. No reason to be alarmed, yet Scott was uneasy about the missing deckhand.

The ship fell behind the jetty, and only the topsails stuck out over the small rise of land. Scott trained the glasses on the schooner's aftertrail, tracked the clean white wake all the way back to Goose Island. Nothing. Still, he couldn't shake the feeling someone or something had gone over the side and been swallowed up in the sea. Stupid, no good reason, probably, but he wanted another look. It was fairly common this time of the evening for the northbound sailing ships to drop the hook in Griffin Bay just outside Fish Creek, behind the Cape.

He raced the Jeep on the winding road to Fish Creek, but when he reached the small opening overlooking Griffin Bay, the strange ship was nowhere in sight. He counted four sloops and a ketch anchored near the fish-buyer's barge and a half-dozen cruisers, lying outside the creek.

Scott was confident he'd spot the tall masts headed north up San Juan Channel, but the fog, now moving quietly into the bay, had already covered the passage all the way north to Lopez Head. Scott stared up the slot into nothingness and shook his head in disgust. It was that kind of day, everything inside out and imagination set to run wild.

Had he been thinking about Owen lying there in a pool of his own blood, the face masked in death, or was it Toni? He was doing it again. When he thought he'd seen a man fall off the stern of that ship, he was really only seeing Toni in her big yellow Mercedes, crashing through the barriers, flying off the end of the ferry landing pitched forward and falling, sinking deep, drowning in the cold waters of the sound.

Three

Scott always looked forward to his evenings with the professor. The old man lived by himself with Chips, a small gray terrier, and a cat, a long-haired, rather frightening creature called Archimedes. Al's wife had passed on years before. Except for a granddaughter who visited on occasion, this was all the family the old man had left.

He was bundled up in a coat sweater over a flannel shirt, stoking up the fire in the stone fireplace when Scott and Dandy arrived. It must have been eighty in the room. "C'mon in, Scottie. Just thought I'd get the chill out of the night air."

In shirtsleeves himself, Scott smiled and set his parcels on the kitchen drain. "Here are the steaks. Thought we could throw them on the barbecue."

The old man nodded. "I'll toss some lettuce in a bowl. Sit yourself down, and I'll fix us a drink."

Glad to see his friend in a lighter mood, Scott dropped into a chair. Dandy had already found a cool spot by the window next to Chips. The more aloof cat sat on a table near the hearth, cleaning itself. Scott settled back with a sigh.

The place was bachelor simple: a sofa; soft, bulging cushions, the kind to sink in; and a scuffed green leather chair Scott had long coveted. For Scott, who'd been living in the Seattle town house with Louis XV chairs and Grecian sofas, it was the ultimate in comfort and sensibility. The whole room was like that. A desk held the professor's beat-up old Underwood. Books jammed an entire wall; some were stacked around the floor, as well. "Been meaning to get some more shelves for those," Al said, dismissing the mess as unimportant.

The professor worked at the sink, chipping ice cubes out of the tray with a knife. He poured from a bottle of Gordon's, added a splash of tonic, and stirred with the knife. "Saw Leroy over at your place. Anything new?"

Scott took the glass from his hand and swirled the cubes. "Apparently one of the African masks was missing from the bedroom."

"He raced over here to tell you that?"

"That, and to thank me, I guess."

"Leroy? Thank you? Look out! He's after something."

Scott sipped the tonic and said nothing.

"He doesn't think they killed Owen over a jungle mask, I hope."

"Those masks are worth a lot, Al."

"Pure nonsense. They wouldn't have left the rest of the junk."

Scott conceded the point. With thousands of dollars of statues and artifacts lying around for the taking, why would a thief bother with only one mask? "At least we can rule out the people on the Cape. We're pretty much a live-and-let-live bunch. No nuts. No psychopaths."

Al laughed.

"Don't you agree?"

Al brandished his drink like a pointer at a chalkboard. "People on this Cape are exactly the same as people everywhere—same problems, same frustrations, same passions."

Scott grinned back at him. "You don't think one of our neighbors walked into Owen's living room, unloaded two barrels into his chest, and, casual as you please, strolled back home."

"There are more people around here than you might expect who won't shed a tear at Owen's passing."

"How about a for instance?"

"Henry Mason."

Scott couldn't picture the Cape's only multimillionaire

tightening his arthritic fingers on the trigger of a shotgun. "What possible reason?"

"Owen borrowed money from Henry and managed to write a loophole in the contract so he didn't have to pay back a cent."

Scott laughed. "I underestimated Owen. I thought ol' Henry had his first nickel."

"That's what I mean. Henry isn't the sort to allow a four-flusher like Owen to get the better of him. And Henry's not alone. You talk to Vic recently?"

"Three or four days ago," Scott said guardedly.

"Did he tell you about the West Coast fish deal?"

"He said they'd gone under, and he hoped to get better prices from the new fish-buyer."

The crinkles around Al's eyes deepened. "Did he tell you Owen talked him into investing in West Coast just before they filed for Chapter Eleven?"

"Owen sucked Vic into that?"

Al nodded. "Vic lost a bundle."

Vic Larson was the owner of a string of purse seiners, and in his time had made a small fortune fishing. The trouble now, the fishermen had come upon bad times with the restrictions placed on their fishing rights by the government, and their seasons were shorter and leaner. Scott counted Vic among his closest friends, and the idea he'd suffered a financial setback at the hands of Owen upset him. "Vic's not your man, Al."

"How about Bob Delaney? Owen cheated him out of a big real estate commission. From what I hear, Delaney was so hopping mad, he threatened to kill Owen."

Scott shook his head on the idea. Delaney bordered on being the town drunk. "It takes a certain kind of nerve to empty a twelve-gauge into a man, Al. Delaney doesn't have it."

Al played a Beethoven sonata on his stereo, and, after dinner, with the fire hissing and snapping in the grate, they retreated to the living room. Al poured coffee, a wonderful brew he boiled in an open pot, and complained about the aging process that robbed a man of the joys of life.

Scott's gaze fell on his friend's telescope, which sat by the windows, aimed at Cattle Pass. "Did you catch the schooner that went through this afternoon?"

"Mmm. The *Pilgrim.* Beautiful job."

"You've seen her before?"

Al nodded. "Charter ship. Last summer the Sea Scouts had her. This year it's the experimental lab. They use her to test the quality of the water, or some such nonsense."

"Kind of an expensive job for that." This touched off a lengthy sermon from Al on university waste. Satisfied the old man had seen nothing, Scott said, "How's the book coming?"

Al grunted disinterest, but from the typewritten pages scattered across his desk, it appeared he'd been working diligently on his history of the islands.

"Must be fun researching the misadventures of renegades and smugglers," Scott said. "Islands have quite a past."

"Do you imagine it's changed?"

Scott laughed. "You're not going to tell me they're still hijacking ships and that sort of skulduggery."

"Shows how much you know. If you've been reading the papers, there's been a half-dozen ships pirated in these islands in the last year alone. Forced a couple off their cruiser at gunpoint up near Campbell River. Took them two days to flag a passing ship."

"At least no one was hurt."

"That'll be next." From this typically gloomy view, Al launched into stories about the early San Juan settlers who'd come around the Horn. From this he branched into ancient Greece. Although Scott had heard much of it before, he was fully absorbed.

"You're quite a storyteller, Al. Why don't you go back to teaching? Guest lecture, something like that?"

"All those department heads climbing on top of each other to get to the top of the monkey tree? Don't want any part of it." That ended the conversation.

"How long you been up here on the Cape, Al?"

"Going on twelve years."

"Do you ever miss, uh, being away from things?"

"Spit it out, for heaven's sake. No, I don't mind being alone, if that's what you're getting at." He walked over to the fire and poked at a log. "'Course, I have Chips and Archimedes. They're good company. And these darn fool people around here are always popping in, never know when to leave a person alone. And there's Erin." He doffed his pipe stem at a picture on the top of his desk of a fair-haired girl with blue eyes, even, white teeth, and a smile that suggested a happy outlook.

All Scott could remember about Al's granddaughter from previous summers was a pleasant, long-legged teenager who asked too many questions and was fascinated by the fishing boats. He hadn't seen her at all in the last few years when his own life had been too complicated for him to spend much time on the island. So he more or less missed a part of her growing up. "I imagine Erin's in college now."

Al grinned. "Where you been? She's been out of college nearly five years. She's a decorator. Tells people how to doll up their homes." He chuckled. "She's got her eye on my place, calls it a challenge. I tell her hands off."

Scott groaned. "Don't let her touch a thing, Al. Your place is perfect."

It was late when Scott finally asked what had been on his mind all evening. "When Toni came up those last times, was she alone?"

"She had a guest or two. Lorene dropped by, and the Martins. I ran into her on the beach a few times myself."

"How did she seem to you?"

"Preoccupied."

Scott remembered her moods of silence. "Those parties of Owen's—did you ever hear of her going?"

Al grabbed the poker stick and dug at a log that had flamed up, shoved it to the back of the firebox. "All hearsay, you understand, but someone did mention he'd seen her there, talking to that bird who works at the experimental lab, the dark-haired slicker. You know who I mean?"

"Preston Fields."

"That's the one."

It was like going the wrong direction on a one-way street. Scott knew Fields, never liked him. He thought Toni had felt the same. "What do you know about him, Al?"

"Oceanographer, biologist, hotshot. Got his Ph.D. before he was thirty. A Rhodes scholar. Comes from wealth. Arrogant, self-impressed, and sneaky. I think that about covers it." Al smiled.

But Scott couldn't laugh, for he felt the same way about the man, and the idea of Toni taking up with Preston depressed him.

Al read his thoughts. "I said she was *seen* there with him. Doesn't have to mean she came with him."

Scott nodded and decided if Al knew more, he didn't want to know.

Four

Friday Harbor was the usual summer mess, boats and tourists everywhere, as Scott and Dandy pulled in. Cars, campers, vans, bicycles, and mopeds clogged the three blocks of the main street, and in the harbor, cruisers and sailboats filled up the docks behind the breakwater and overflowed to anchorage across half the bay.

Al had a meeting of his historical society, and in a weak moment, Scott volunteered to pick Erin up from the noon ferry, an offer he already regretted. "C'mon, Dandy," Scott said, piling out of the Jeep, "let's get this over with."

He had no trouble picking Erin out of the crowd of foot passengers milling around the ferry hut. She was the tall, healthy-looking young woman with shoulder-length blond hair holding on to a two-suiter and a backpack. Up close, she was as he remembered, no more freckles across the bridge of her nose, but soft features, inquisitive eyes, and a brilliant smile. The gentle curves and a certain matureness in her direct gaze were new.

She squeezed in beside Dandy in the front seat of the Jeep, and they started out. Their conversation quickly turned to her profession, and he made the mistake of expressing his views that the decorators he'd known had been more concerned with putting their artistic stamp on a house than with the people who had to live in it. It was an opinion formed because of Toni, of course, and unfair, but Erin took it well.

"It's not quite like you think," she said. "You have to study your clients and work to achieve a mood they want." It was, she said, a combination of psychology and crossword puzzles. "You have to start with what's given and go from there." She talked about trade-offs and getting to know the people you're working for and architectural limits and the use of space, and Scott soon realized there was more to it than he'd thought.

In a fenced stretch along the road, a small herd of goats was at work pulling up the tall grass. Beyond the field, yellowed pastures layered the hillside all the way to the tide pools of Griffin Bay.

"I suppose," Scott said, still not completely convinced, "that you prefer the kind of job where someone gives you the key to the house and a checkbook and tells you to do whatever you like."

The wind from the open window blew the fine golden strands of hair into her eyes. She brushed them back. "There's no challenge in that, not to have to please anyone, no wish lists."

"Wish lists?"

"A family heirloom or an exotic teapot, a painting or a special color." She flashed the smile again, a very nice smile. "The idea is to bring all those personal desires together into a harmonious whole so you get the home the people wanted all along."

How, he wondered, could she have managed it with two who disagreed as much as he and Toni had? There hadn't been a comfortable chair in the place, and rooms so orderly even the copy of his surgery journal on a desktop looked out of place.

"You might not believe it," she said in a spirited voice that bordered on defense, "but I'm actually pretty damn good at what I do."

He liked her self-confidence, imagined she was, indeed, good at what she did. He also imagined she could manipulate a man with her smile and soft voice. Make certain it's not you she manipulates, he warned himself. He drove over a hill and fell in behind a long line of cyclers, pedaling earnestly toward American Camp. An irrigated field on the hill glistened emerald green against the straw slopes around it. Griffin Bay opened up again across the yellowed thickets of grass.

The road curved through the woods by American Camp, and the fields turned into stands of newly planted pine, spruce, and firs. Erin breathed deeply of the air. "Wild berries and pine needles. I used to dream about those marvelous smells. I spent entire summers here before college, after the accident."

Scott remembered when she lost her parents. He hadn't known Al at the time, but Al told him about it later, the fiery crash on the mountain road. At first Erin and Al had clung to each other like nesting swallows. Then, gradually, they'd come out of it, but the bond between them remained. Thinking of Erin's loss, Scott felt a sudden bond with her himself. "You were very young to lose your parents."

She shrugged. "I was fifteen, but I was lucky. I had Grandpa."

Somehow the notion of Al playing mother and father to a girl in her delicate growing years didn't fit. Still, Scott could see his friend had done a remarkably good job. She had survived with a fatalistic acceptance that did Al credit. "You didn't stay on the island for school?"

"No. Grandpa sent me to boarding school in Canada, but I stayed close to home for college. Grandpa's getting on, you know."

"Mmm," Scott said, suddenly feeling old.

The road dipped and rolled. The grass slopes of Mount Finlayson had turned into a parched bog, tinder dry. Fire warnings had been out for days. Erin's eyes followed the movements of a hawk who appeared to be suspended over the swirling blue eddies of the strait. Below them a white surf was running, and across the wide expanse of shimmering water, the Olympic Mountains stood in a misty outline against a sun-hazed sky.

The road wound around Finlayson and opened up a view of the lighthouse and the string of small islands that clustered across Cattle Pass. A wind had started up, and big rollers put a spray over Deadman's Island that Scott guessed rose over fifty feet in the air. It was a smashing sight, and never failed to restore him. Erin leaned out the window to get a better look. A flock of gulls flew by, squealing like a crowd of frightened puppies.

Erin released a deep sigh. "If I came here a million times, I'd never get over the feeling. It's such a joy to see, just to know it's there."

In that moment she closed the age gap, and in this state of rapport, they drove the next half-mile, hypnotized into silence by the sight of the whirling waters and the tiny islands that strung out from the toe of Lopez. At the bend in the road where the grass had grown over the sandy trail to the lighthouse, they passed the blockhouse, freshly painted. Here, in the Second World War, sailors had protected the coast with a giant radar net and used the concrete building as a radar station and pillbox. Now it lay empty, with holes for windows and doors, a place for the tourists to crawl through.

The road dipped one more time, and out of a grove of leafy ash and madronas, Owen's skylighted roof pitched above the trees. Erin had heard about Owen. "Isn't it awful, knowing someone was killed here in this breathtaking spot? Gives you a terrible feeling, not just that a killer is loose, but the whole idea of someone violating this beautiful place. I hate that especially. Do you know what I mean?"

He knew exactly. Evil had touched the Cape, and it didn't belong there.

Erin was on the island for her vacation, and Al made such a point of Scott's coming to her "homecoming dinner" that he couldn't refuse. It was amusing to see her influence on the old man. Al wasn't what Scott called a moody person. Still, living alone he could go for days communicating in monosyllables. Tonight, he was in exceptional humor and talkative as a jay.

Erin was in the kitchen preparing dessert when he dropped one of his little bombs. He'd run into Leroy's deputy in town. "They found the missing death mask. According to Harold, some bird sold it to an antique dealer in Victoria."

Erin walked back into the room carrying a large bowl of strawberries. "Did I hear you say something about Owen's African art collection?"

Al came up in his chair. "What do you know about it?"

"Didn't I tell you? I saw some of his collection last summer."

Al sucked in his breath and looked like he might explode. "You went to one of Owen's parties?"

"I didn't say that, Grandpa. What do you take me for?"

"A girl with a nose for other people's business," Al said, a little less excited.

"I was walking back from the lighthouse," Erin explained, "and Owen came out for his morning jog. He stopped me, said he'd heard I was an interior decorator and asked if I knew anything about African artifacts. Of course, I'd done some work for clients. Anyway, there was nothing suggestive about it. He merely wanted my professional opinion."

"And Owen's stuff? Is it very valuable?" Scott said.

Erin nodded. "Besides the fact that the wood is highly perishable in the tropics, the trible customs discouraged preservation of ritual masks, so those that come through a few centuries, like Owen's, are rare and dearly priced. As for the terra-cotta head, it probably dates back to two or three hundred B.C."

Impressed by her knowledge, Scott said, "I read recently that some art dealers were making a killing selling fake Dali prints for thousands of dollars."

Erin nodded. "You can imagine the problem in African art with centuries of artifacts to deal with. But Owen's were of high quality, the material old, the color good. I'd say whoever picked them knew what he was doing."

"You don't think it was Owen?"

Erin shook her head. "When he showed me the ivory piece he didn't even know what century it came from. I suggested he consult the museum curator in Seattle if he wanted to be absolutely certain, but he didn't like that idea at all. I wouldn't be surprised if the terra-cotta head was worth a quarter of a million."

Scott whistled. "A quarter of a million bucks sitting on a table in a summerhouse."

"It figgers," Al said. "Owen was an operator and a cheat, but an intellect he was not."

Erin laughed. "That's nothing. The chain he wore around his neck was a museum piece."

Scott exchanged glances with Al. "Damn," Scott said. "How could I have forgotten those bilious gold sticks hanging down his bare chest like a Tahitian witch doctor? Better call the sheriff, Al. He'll want to know about that."

Erin looked puzzled.

"It wasn't on him when we found the body," Al explained.

Leroy responded with uncharacteristic swiftness. He rumbled up the drive, strode through Al's door, wearing the Stetson and the .38, and there was an uncommon look of urgency on his face. He saw Erin and removed the hat, brushed life back into the thin matted brown hair, and shifted from one foot to the other while Al explained about Erin and the necklace.

"How valuable is it?" Leroy asked Erin.

"Taking a guess . . . twenty-five thousand. To be sure, you'd have to ask an authority, which I'm really not."

Leroy pulled at an earlobe. "Do you know such a person?"

"The museum curator in Seattle, for one. I also know a collector, a client of mine, who's made it his hobby. Brice Randall, the Seattle developer. You may have heard of him."

Small damn world, Scott thought. Who hadn't heard of Randall, the contractor who'd built shopping malls and office complexes all over the Northwest? Scott knew him from Toni's store parties, met him first at the opening of one of Randall's malls. He wasn't a physically big man, but he had a forceful personality. Meeting him was like being hit by a strong wind. He was quick, always knew just the right thing to say.

"I decorated his offices in the Pacific building a year ago," Erin told Leroy. "We designed a whole room around pieces he picked up in auctions."

Leroy whipped out his notepad and began writing on it. He looked up once and saw Scott's frown. "You ever see Owen wearing the necklace?"

Scott nodded unhappily. "Yes, I've seen it on him, and, no, it wasn't on him when I examined him, and yes, it only now occurred to me."

Leroy shrugged. "You can't think of everything."

Al, who'd been strangely quiet through all this, said, "Your deputy tells me you found the missing African mask."

Leroy frowned. "Harold talks too much."

Al bit down on his pipe irritably.

Leroy had investigated the guests at Owen's party, most of whom were now living out of the state. None of the ladies held any regret at Owen's passing.

This evoked a sympathetic "Poor man!" from Erin.

"Ummmph," Al said, meaning Owen deserved whatever he got.

"But he wasn't lucky at marriage, was he? A man without friends."

His eyes on Erin, Leroy left them with a warning. "Better not talk it around, this business of Owen and the necklace."

Al drew up like a rooster. "Leroy, are you telling my granddaughter she's in danger because she saw Owen's collection of African art?"

Leroy turned his serious gaze on the old man. "I'm saying when you're dealing with a deranged killer, it pays to be careful. The fewer people who know what you know, the better."

Five

After Leroy left, Scott started across the road to his house in the dark. Forgot his yard lights. The Martins' lights were out, too. He glanced at his watch. Two-thirty. Tonight he knew he'd sleep, sleep without the gremlins of Toni and Owen, and the promise of it filled him with a peace he hadn't known in weeks.

Off Goose Island the moon spun a white trail across the kelp bed. From the Cattlepoint rocks the lighthouse lamp flickered on and off, and another answered. There was an occasional cry from a wayward gull, and then silence. Stars overhead blinked back mutely, and not an engine rumbled anywhere. It was one of those peaceful nights on the Cape when even the tide slipped in quietly.

Dandy spotted it first, the long shadow darting across the grass by the corner of the house. With a low growl, he left the road at a gallop, headed toward the rocks below the deck.

It's hard to prepare oneself for combat on such a night, and it was pure reflex that sent Scott running across the road behind Dandy. The memory of Leroy's warnings brought a shout from his lips. "Hey, what's going on here?" His voice shattered the silence like the Cape's fire horn, and a sorry second thought followed. Probably the Martins' tabby, Sam, getting another lick off Dandy's dish.

Fresh scuffling sounds, definitely not the soft scampering of a cat. Someone was coming out of his house. Another shadow limped off the deck, Dandy in rumbling pursuit.

"C'mon, Charlie," someone shouted, "let's get the hell outta here."

"Watch out for the fuckin' dog. . . ."

Scott raced to the deck and whistled to Dandy, but the dog was already thundering across the hard turf, charging over the logs and rocks on the heels of the intruders. Scott reached the mound above the beach, close enough to hear their grunting exertions. The light was too poor to make out faces but he had had time to consider the very real possibility that men who break into other people's homes quite likely also carry guns. He stepped lightly across the grass and whistled again for the dog, but received only Dandy's bark in answer.

If they'd run to the beach, Scott reasoned, they must have a way of escape by water, but if he ran after them he'd be an easy target. Scott knew every inch of the beach, knew where the driftwood piled up in a long chain, sticking out like giant toothpicks, and where the mammoth first-growth fir, stripped of its bark and slippery as a seal's skin, lay like a teeter-totter over the top. Nestled in between the stumps and logs that had been cast there by earlier storms was a pebbled stretch of beach, sometimes turned to sand by a high tide. In this spot he and Toni had basked together in the sun, made love in the shelter of the driftwood. Here the rocks formed a small cove with a tide pool in its center. There was a sand strip between the jetties where a small boat could slip into shore, and, if tied to a rock in a gentle sea, like tonight, could sit on the mud bottom, free of trouble.

Close to the bank, footsteps crunched across the hard sand. Dandy lunged through the dark at two figures scrambling for the logs. Barking fiercely, Dandy forced them up against the big fir where they stood on the poles underneath and began fending the dog off with kicks and karate chops.

"Hold him off. I'll get the line." The shorter of the two, the one called Charlie, left the protection of the tree and loped across the beach, stumbled over a rock, regained his footing, and hobbled to the mushy sand at the water's edge where a small boat sat tied to the rocks. There he began unsnarling the boat's line, which appeared to be fouled in a heavy patch of seaweed.

The stick-shaped man by the tree dropped to a squat,

groped around between the logs. "Get back, you bastard, or I'll fix you good." His hand rested on a thick piece of driftwood. He raised the hunk of wood at the dog like a club, and brought it down with savage force. It struck a large rock and splintered, missing Dandy, but not, Scott figured, by much.

"Dandy," Scott shouted, starting to panic. "Dandy!"

Normally Dandy would have come at this command, and normally he would have been content to chase the intruders off as he would the neighbor's cat, with a good deal of barking and growling. But this man had lashed back so viciously that the dog sensed he was a threat and turned mean. He went after the man with the club, snarling and snapping, not actually biting but keeping him pinned against the tree.

"Shit, stand still, you bastard." The man with the club raised it, swung, missed, swung again.

Scott leaned over the bank. "Knock it off!"

Neither the man nor Dandy paid the least attention. How, Scott wondered fearfully, was he to get Dandy safely out of there without taking on these men himself? As he stood over them weighing his options, he saw the man's hand slide inside his jacket. The unmistakable sound of a .38 chamber slamming into place chilled the air.

"I'll fix the son of a bitch."

Too late for help. Too late for argument. Scott leaped over the rock embankment to the beach, landed on his feet, and knew in the splash of cool air from the water that he'd done the dumbest thing possible. On the bank the two men were merely vandals in flight, but here, down on the sand, they were fury locked in a small room. The fear for Dandy had prompted him to do what all reason warned against. Scott's throat muscles constricted. The words when they came out sounded like they were coming out of frozen lips. "Shoot that dog and you'll be sorry. I promise you."

The head turned, and Scott saw black, tightly curled hair, a face blotted out by darkness, and the nose of the automatic, trained on his chest. The man holding it laughed. It wasn't a pleasant laugh. It wasn't a pleasant feeling, staring down the barrel of a loaded automatic in the hands of a man intent on using it. "You want it first?"

From the water's edge, "Charlie" paused in his work. "Jerry, you stupid bastard, put it away!"

"If he doesn't get this fuckin' dog off me, I'll put them both away for good."

"*Dandy, come!*" The dog knew the voice of serious command. He returned to Scott's side, panting. His whole body quivered.

Scott faced them both now—Charlie, the short scruffy one struggling to unsnarl the line that was hung up in the kelp, and his partner, the one called Jerry, who still held the automatic, still, apparently, undecided what he would do with it. In the dark their faces were blurs, but their hate charged across the beach like a broken high-power line.

"That's right!" Jerry said. No mistaking the madness in that voice. "Keep that mutt off me, or I'll blow his brains all over the beach."

Scott took a firm hold on Dandy's collar. Close by, the man near the boat managed to undo the lines, and, in one swift motion, was in the boat, working to get it started. He turned the key, choked it. The engine sputtered, quit. He snapped the key another time with the same result. He tried it again and again.

"Hurry it up, will you?"

"It's not getting gas. Oh, shit—dammit to hell."

The obscenities showered from the cockpit as Charlie hand-pumped fuel through the hose. There would, Scott thought, be no better opportunity to move, to see what they'd taken from the house. He took a step toward them. The stringy shadow shot up in front of him.

"That's far enough."

"Now look," Scott said, trying reason, "what do you want here?"

Laughter, cruel and wild, pealed out of the shadows.

Scott advanced another step. It was a mistake.

The automatic came up. "Fuck off!"

The gun, the words hurled with the unchecked anger of the insane, worked at Dandy's instincts to protect. The dog pulled free. Everything exploded at once. Dandy dove, and the gun went off, cracked across the water like an engine backfiring on a quiet street. Jerry went down, and the gun spit loose, sailed across the sand. Dandy landed on top, snarling, biting, and this time, Scott feared, tearing flesh. Scott raced in, got a handhold on Dandy's fur, and with his free hand grabbed the collar, pulled with all his might. Dandy's teeth let go their hold, and Scott dragged him off. Jerry had crawled behind the log, curled up in a ball, protecting his face with his arms.

"You son of a bitch. I'll get you." Spitting out mouthfuls of sand and kelp, he crawled out from under the log and scratched at the ground. He was after the gun, dropped somewhere in the piles of rock, mud, and seaweed. He was near crazy, digging and clawing. Finally his fingers curled around the only weapon he could find. He struggled to his feet, getting his breath in stuttering heaves, and started toward Scott, clutching the club, arms upraised, out of control.

Charlie thumped around the bow of their boat, waving a wrench and yelling at his companion, "Don't, you damn fool." Dandy broke loose. Scott saw the club going up, coming down. He moved. It wasn't quite far enough. The club missed his head, struck his shoulder, a stinging, staggering blow. He reeled back, pain radiating all the way up his neck and down his arm to his fingertips, jarred from his chest to his toes. He fell into mud, fighting to keep his equilibrium. The beach started to spin. Above him, through half-open eyes, Scott saw the club go up one more time.

Teeth bared, Dandy sprang from the pebbled patch of beach, a hundred pounds of solid, straining muscles, aimed, on target. But this time Jerry was ready. He didn't miss. The club slammed into the dog's side. Dandy flew across the sand and landed with a thud, his whimpering cry dying in the back reaches of the bank.

In a dazed state, Scott saw the boat float free in the tide

pool, then the burst of horsepower as the engine caught hold, sputtered, and throttled into a roar. It was a Whaler, a fast boat, revved up, ready to go. Anger choked up in Scott's throat. Fighting waves of dizziness, he staggered to his feet, stumbled after them.

"Get in," he heard the driver shout to his companion.

Club still in hand, Jerry half-somersaulted over the bow into the boat. Scott grabbed the bow plate. It was round and smooth, hard to grip, but he held on. If he'd stopped to think, he would have known it was a futile gesture against two hundred horses of powerful outboard. But he was past thinking.

The club rose like a heavy hunk of steel, and he heard the sharp intake of breath—his own—and the laugh of this man who so enjoyed inflicting pain. Until now Scott had been moving at half speed, impeded by the burning in his shoulder and the wooziness. But when it came to protecting his hands, he had good reflexes. The club dropped. Scott unzipped his fingers. Plastic cracked. Scott fell facedown into mud and seaweed with the sickening crunch of splintering fiberglass grinding in his ears, and the knowledge that crept into his consciousness that, had the club struck its target, it wouldn't have been the plastic parapet crushed and pulverized, but the bones in his fingers, the surgeon's hands crippled.

Lying in the sand, Scott watched the driver of the Whaler back it up, turn, nose into a wave, and shove the stick forward. The small boat, bow up, lifted off its sandy slip, bounced over its own wake, and, spinning a silver tail, planed across an otherwise quiet sea on a reckless course up San Juan Channel. The engine rumbled into the distance and left the Cape in silence.

Scott dragged himself to the slippery log, his heart heavy with remorse. He scanned the rocks where he'd last heard Dandy's pitiful yelp. Nothing. It was all his fault. If he'd only held on to the dog, not provoked the fury of the intruders. Nothing those two could have taken from the house was worth a hair of Dandy's head. With dread, he called the dog's name. A wave splashed across the pebbles and fell softly back.

"Where are you, boy?" he called as he inched across the sand, testing the ground with his toes, afraid of what he might find. He found nothing. He started for the house to get a flashlight.

At first it sounded only like the tide coming in.

"Dandy?"

This time there was a faint scuffling sound to raise his hopes. It came out of the logjam at the foot of the rocks just below the deck. He called again.

The answering whimper gave fresh life to Scott's sore limbs. He ran to the logs, fearful and hoping at the same time. The whimper turned into a sharp bark, and Scott's spirits soared. He ran his hand through the gaps in the pile and touched the soft tufts of fur. A warm tongue ran over his hand, and Scott wanted to cry out in relief. Dandy was wedged between two logs, squirming frantically to get out, and from all appearances, still in one piece.

The logs were big and firmly set and hard to budge, and Scott wondered how the dog had been trapped there. The only thing Scott could imagine was that, when struck, he had landed on the pile, slipped on the slick surface of the wet wood, and slid between the poles, causing the top ones to settle in around him.

"Don't worry, boy, I'll have you out in a minute."

Using his good shoulder, Scott got under the top log and managed to work it up and to the side. Still not enough. He needed to move the one underneath, but this was cedar, water-soaked, and heavy. If he dislodged the wrong pole, it might bring the pile down on top of the dog. Scott took a deep breath and went at it again. But he needed leverage, not brawn. He stumbled across the beach until he found a pole, just the right size. He placed it under the cedar log and pressed down. The log inched up.

"Come on, boy, help."

Dandy needed no encouragement. He wiggled, shoved, clawed, and finally burst free. The pole snapped up and spit out, and the logs tumbled back into place. Exhausted, Scott fell to the sand. He was close to weeping. He wrapped his arms around the dog's neck. Never had that thick bundle of hair felt so good.

Dandy licked his face and whined and pranced around like a puppy, answering Scott's fears about broken limbs and injured inner organs. With the heavy padding of fur and fat, he'd been stunned, nothing more.

"We're tougher than we think, ol' boy."

Bruised muscles and injured pride—they were much better off than they might have been. No bullets had flown, Scott thought gratefully, and he and Dandy were still alive and on their feet. "C'mon," Scott said, "let's see what they did to the house."

Six

The house was a mess. Sofa cushions, coats, and jackets all over the floor, linings ripped, kindling from the wood box splintering the rug. In the kitchen, cupboards stood empty. On the floor broken pieces of china lay buried in a sea of sugar and flour beside drawers, turned upside down, with silverware and fishing tackle spilling out.

The den was the worst, books thrown around and medical papers ripped out of files. Scott retrieved a red leather-bound copy of Shakespeare's *Sonnets* and let out a soft "Damn!" It had been a gift from Toni on their anniversary. It looked like a bird with a broken wing.

Anger turned to gloom as Scott waded through the rooms. They'd ransacked his bureau drawers, stripped the bed, and tossed sheets, blankets, socks, shirts, slacks, underwear, and towels into one big pile. The bathroom reeked of after-shave. A broken bottle of it leaked onto the tile. Clearly, Charlie and Jerry had been intent on doing as much mischief as possible. Strangely, a bottle of Demerol prescribed for Toni when she had root-canal work done lay unopened on the floor.

Apparently, he'd interrupted the two before they'd finished in the living room. His surprise arrival had spared the loss of his ship models, the oil seascape that hung over the hearth, his stereo, and his shortwave. Even more amazing, not one bottle of wine had been dislodged from its rack over the kitchen pass-through.

It was too early to be certain, but upon first look there appeared, in fact, to be nothing missing, which made no sense. If they weren't thieves, who were these men, and what had they been after? They were too old to be vandals. Could the break-in be tied in with Owen? If so, had it anything to do with Toni?

He went back to the bedroom, dug through the underwear and the socks, and found the few remnants of Toni he'd saved— her evening bag, the photograph album, her Sunday missal. Sighing heavily, Scott telephoned the sheriff.

Leroy didn't sound cheered by the news of another problem on the Cape. "Just took my shoes off."

"I don't think I'm missing anything," Scott said, "so there's nothing urgent about it."

"Umm. They got away clean?"

"At those speeds they could be in Canada by now."

"All right," Leroy said, "I'll stop out in the morning and see if we can lift some prints. Try not to touch anything."

Scott didn't remember the .38 until he put down the phone. There seemed to be no point in calling the sheriff again, but he knew the gun might be a means of identifying the two, and it was somewhere on that beach. With another half hour to high tide, there was the chance of losing it to an outgoing wave.

Scott dug out the big flashlight and, every muscle protesting, trudged wearily back to the beach. Dandy limped loyally behind him. Scott shone the torch in all the likely and unlikely places, into the crevices between the rocks, around the fir near where the thug had stood, poked it into the hollowed-out ends of logs, under stacks of driftwood. He shoveled seaweed with his foot. Dandy helped, digging and pawing the sand. They uncovered nothing. Scott finally concluded the gun was either tucked between the logs or buried in a tide pool. In either case, there was no way he'd find it in the dark. He gave up and, thoroughly exhausted, returned to the house, hopeful he'd uncover it in the morning at low tide.

He swept the broken dishes into one big pile in the center of the kitchen. The rest, he decided, could wait until morning. He threw sheets on the bed and, totally drained from his efforts, fell onto it.

Lights from across the water blinked on and off into his

room. After his struggle on the beach it was inevitable that his mind go back in time, seeing it all as though it had happened minutes ago. Fred at the door, his face as gray as the early-hour fog that brought him.

"Toni's dead, Scottie."

Scott could still see her lying lifeless under the pathologist's thin cloth, palid and puffed up from the salt water, looking defenseless. Toni, who'd always been in control of everything. He remembered thinking he ought to cover her with his coat, and the police sergeant saying, "You'll want this, I imagine." It was Toni's black evening bag. The policeman had spilled its water-soaked contents out on the table—her lip gloss, compact, comb, keys, wallet, and the small appointment book she took with her everywhere. There was no living relative, only Scott, to receive it. Scott had stared at it bleakly. Not much to show for thirty-five years of life.

"C'mon, Scottie," Fred said, "you can't do anything here."

The house had a deep-winter chill when he returned to it that night, damp and emptier than the day she'd left, and he couldn't stand to stay in it. For hours he drifted down mist-blotted streets, staring blindly at the hazy outlines of unlit homes, unable to get the sight of her from his mind.

It was something like that now, except for the first time since that cold November night, other thoughts raced through his head as he lay staring into the darkness: Owen and the marine biologist Preston Fields, Owen and the fishermen, Owen and Toni, and then, strangely, like a warm wind coming after a blizzard, Erin and the way she looked when she said, ". . . the idea of someone violating this beautiful place . . . I hate that. . . ."

He finally fell into a fitful sleep, interrupted by questions too disturbing to chase away. Why had Toni gone to Owen's parties? Why had she driven through the barricade? Toni, whose only real fear in life was of the water? What happened at the store opening to drive her off that way? The coroner called it an accident and, privately, said suicide, but Scott knew Toni and could accept neither theory. In the predawn darkness, the glow from the lighthouse flickered on and off. If he found the reasons for Owen's death, would he also discover the truth about Toni? As the sun poked over Mount Baker, Scott drifted off to sleep.

He woke abruptly again with the ringing of the phone. It was Fred, calling from Seattle, and he sounded excited. "Scottie, where you been? I tried to reach you for hours last night. What's going on up there, anyway? The papers say someone shot Owen. Do they know who?"

Scott raised himself to one elbow and mumbled into the receiver. "Oh, hi, Fred." Fred went right on talking.

"Why didn't you call me? That's right next door, you know."

"Don't know who did it or why," Scott said through a yawn, and told Fred what he knew.

"Good God, I wonder if they've checked our house. Who's handling it, anyway?"

"Leroy. And don't worry, he checked your place first thing. Nothing was touched. You know I would've told you had it been otherwise."

Sounding slightly mollified, Fred said, "It sounds like we've got a maniac running loose up there."

Scott yawned again. "If that's the case, if it's not the work of a thief, your house is perfectly safe."

"Yeah," Fred said, not laughing and not sounding reassured either. Finally he said, "See you in a day or so. Oh, Lorene says she'll work something out with Cynthia."

Scott groaned. "I don't want her to work something out with Cynthia."

Fred laughed. "If you expect me to intervene for you, ol' buddy, forget it."

Scott set the phone down with an annoyed sigh. It was a good five minutes before he realized he hadn't told Fred about his own break-in. Unintentional or Freudian, it was just as well. It would have sent Fred chasing back on the next ferry.

Scott showered and dressed, ignoring an ache in his head that he wasn't sure was a result of no sleep or the blow on the shoulder. He shoveled debris aside so he could feed Dandy, and marveled at how heartily the dog ate, showing no ill effects from the encounter on the beach.

Scott was picking up broken dishes when Leroy's wagon rolled into the drive. Leroy walked in carrying a valise. There'd been more calls last night, and he was clearly in a bad mood.

"Hope you didn't touch anything. I can't get prints if you mucked it up with your own."

Scott led him to the kitchen and pointed to the cupboards. "The handles, the drawer pulls, the counters—all untouched."

"Arrogant doctors," Leroy mumbled. He started rattling around the kitchen, shaking charcoal powder on the countertops and blowing it all over the place. He proceeded from there to the living room and started on the big circular coffee table.

"My God," Scott protested, "you're destroying my house."

Leroy shrugged. "You want to find those two or not?"

"I'm not sure," Scott said as some of the powder settled on the rug.

"Mmm, got something here. 'Course, could be yours." He blew on the powder, and the imprint of three fingers appeared. He laid a plastic tape over this and lifted it off. He repeated this process several times on the fireplace hearth and the tables. "I'm going to need your prints, too."

"Okay." Scott sighed. "But in the kitchen, please."

Scott submitted to the fingerprinting, and Leroy finally packed up his equipment, took a half-dozen prints with him that he thought might be "possibles," and started for the door. Then Scott remembered about the gun. Leroy's disposition did not improve at the news.

"Why in hell didn't you tell me that last night?"

"I forgot. Anyway, what would you have done? Come out here and crawled through the slime and rocks in the pitch dark? I did that, and came up with sore knees and an aching back for my trouble."

"Okay," Leroy said in a tone of resignation, "let's get it done."

They worked their way across the beach from one log pile to

44

another, poked into all the places Scott had looked before and in some he'd missed. They raked and scooped up wet sand and dipped into the spots where water still collected from the outgoing tide. They found seaweed, an empty beer can, wet rocks, and barnacles, but no .38.

After an hour of this, Leroy shook his head. "You sure this bird didn't pick it up again?"

Scott thought about being knocked flat and, for those several spinning seconds, not seeing or hearing clearly. Could either of them have retrieved the gun while he lay there, dazed? "I suppose it's possible."

Beside his patrol car, Leroy expressed the view that it was, after all, only a break-in. Nothing had been stolen and no one seriously hurt. "Keep it to yourself, though. If the people 'round here get an idea there's a crime spree going, the next thing you know we'll have the whole Cape armed to the teeth and shooting every time a dog barks."

The sheriff wasn't five minutes out of the drive when Scott was forced to break his word. Al appeared at the door, took one look into the kitchen, and blanched visibly. "God almighty, somebody broke in."

There was hardly any way to hide it, so Scott told him the whole story, including Leroy's desire to keep it quiet.

"Won't say a word," Al stuttered. "We got something awfully wrong going on here, Scottie, something awfully wrong."

"And I don't think we need worry Erin with it, do you?"

Al nodded dumbly and dropped down onto a kitchen chair. He looked at the pile of broken dishes and then at the powder covering the counters, and shook his head. "This is a mess. You better call Millie."

"I'm not calling anyone, Al. Leroy wants to keep it quiet, remember?"

"Oh, sure." He didn't say anything for another minute. Then, "These two men, did you ever see them before?"

"Can't be sure. Too dark to see their faces clearly."

"And you think they still have the gun?"

"That's the sheriff's idea, not mine. I figure if they'd picked it up again, they would've used it."

"Then it's still out there somewhere?"

"If it is, it's out to sea by now. We scoured that beach."

Al looked like he had when they'd found Owen—pale and deeply worried. "What do you think it all means?"

"Not sure. I can't find anything missing. They even passed up a five-dollar bill on my dresser. Still, it's clear they were looking for something."

"Do—do you suppose they're the ones who killed Owen, that they were looking for something at Owen's place, and he caught them at it, and they shot him? Maybe they didn't find what they were after and so they came here, and . . ."

But what could Scott have in common with Owen? Toni? Was it something to do with Toni?

Al shook his head. "Doesn't make sense, does it? No connection between you and Owen. Besides, we know the killers took the mask and the necklace. Maybe they're part of a burglary ring."

"Then why didn't they steal anything here?"

Al waved his arm in the direction of the kitchen. "How would you know?"

None of the explanations fit, and Al returned to his original theories, that someone on the Cape had killed Owen, which left no explanation for the break-in, but relieved Al's mind. The two were looking for drugs. Everyone knew doctors kept drugs lying around.

Scott hadn't the heart to tell the old man the only drugs in the house were Toni's Demerol capsules, and that the burglars had left those right in the middle of the bathroom floor.

Seven

Bothered by Al's observations about Vic Larson and the West Coast fish-buyers, Scott decided to pay a visit to Fish Creek. It was so out of character for Vic to fall for one of Owen's questionable business investments that Scott had to believe Vic's finances were far worse than he'd realized.

Behind all the fishermen's financial woes was the State Fishing Commission closures. These posed a special hardship for owners of the big purse seiners, like Vic, whose ships represented investments in the millions. Compounding the problem was the federal court ruling on an old Indian treaty that allotted half the salmon catch to the Indians. In effect, this meant the Indians had three times as many days as fishermen like Vic to make their catch. It was a situation bound to cause trouble. Scott hoped eventually the hatcheries would improve the runs and alleviate the problem, but Vic saw only ruin at the end of the road.

"It'll be the Japanese and the Russians getting all the fish," he predicted gloomily. "This country will go begging."

It wasn't a prospect Scott liked to think about.

Fish Creek sat in the backwash of Griffin Bay, exposed to the north but protected from the worst of the south winds by Mount Finlayson and the sand dunes that stretched from the toe of the tiny inlet to Cattle Pass. The midmorning sun was beginning to heat things up as Scott and Dandy drove up in the Jeep. The *Picaroon*'s single mast poked invitingly over the gates to the south dock. No wind for sail today. It was going to be a scorcher. The air already smelled of dead fish. One of the gill-netters had dumped a load of hake that was piled up on the rocks waiting for the next tide to wash it out.

In the creek, a sprinkling of pleasure cruisers and sailboats lay peacefully at anchor, and the long string of gill-netters and purse seiners were still rafted together along the north finger dock. Not a whisper of wind disturbed the water, and on the fishing boats there was a tomblike quiet that reminded Scott of Sunday morning after the fishermen's usual Saturday-night brawls. But this was still Saturday, and there was a disturbing cheerlessness about it.

Scott expected to see some of the Cape residents whose homes fronted on the creek complaining about last night's noise, but there was no one in sight. There'd been a move afoot on the Cape to get the fishermen out of the creek, a move Scott had fought, in spite of his reluctance to get involved in Cape affairs. There was no denying the fishermen were foul-mouthed and noisy at times, but Scott had crewed with them and knew firsthand what a hard life they lived, made harder by the current problems. They were entitled to blow off a little steam.

Scott climbed out of the Jeep and started across the gravel road toward the docks, Dandy running ahead of him. Even from the road the *Nellie J* was an imposing ship. All wood, the big purse seiner measured a hundred feet or better, and her skiff, made of steel and powered by a big diesel inboard, was a good six feet longer than the *Picaroon*.

Scott reached the rock that stuck up over the ramp and spotted Vic's deeply tanned face coming out of the *Nellie J*'s doghouse. Vic wasn't tall, but he was muscular, with shoulders so straight you could almost see him on a parade ground drilling his old platoon, a marine sergeant's cap set forward on a closely shaved head, his lips set in a determined line.

This morning he had the night's growth of stubble on his cheeks, and the black hair on his chest glistened wet as though he'd just stepped out of the shower. He lit a cigarette and blew a small cloud of smoke into the windless air. He stood there, hunched over the port rail, and stared across the bay. Scott knew the feeling of standing alone on the deck, the water slapping gently against the hull. It wasn't a moment to interrupt.

48

He walked softly toward the ramp. As he grew closer he observed the droop to Vic's shoulders. Concerned, he started down the ramp onto the fishermen's pier, which was separated by another gate from the Cape's own pleasure-boat dock. "Morning!"

Vic looked up, raised a brawny tattooed arm in greeting. "Oh . . . hi, Doc. You heard they shut us down again?"

Scott nodded, and saw, as he'd feared, Vic's face had misery written all over it.

"Yeah, they treat us like yo-yos—give us a day, take it back. Piss on all of them. C'mon aboard. We'll break out a six-pack and shoot the shit."

Scott swung a leg over the *Nellie J*'s rail. Dandy was already bouncing all over the stern deck, his shoulder clearly back to normal. His tail banged against the metal inside rails, sending a rattle across the peaceful cove like the clap of kettledrums. "Easy, Dandy!" Dandy skidded to rest under the skiff.

Georgie Ross, Vic's skiffman, stumbled out of the cabin. His red beard bristled like a broom, and, from the swelling under his half-closed eyelids, Scott guessed young Georgie had most definitely partied late. Georgie carried a large plastic sack that, from the lumpy bulges, looked to be full of empty beer cans. Georgie spotted Dandy and dropped the bag. It hit the deck with a clunk. "Hey, Dandy!"

Dandy squirreled out from under the skiff and bounded like a horse over the fish locker. He and Georgie went down, black fur and red hair rolling around with boots and paws like colliding linemen on a football field. They went on with the game until Dandy had mopped Georgie's whiskered cheeks wet.

Vic grinned at their antics; he had a soft spot for both the boy and the dog. "C'mon, Georgie, you'll wake the neighbors."

The words came too late. The racket woke up the other boats. Facing the *Nellie J*'s bow on the *Mollie O*, Davey Olson cracked the hatch open, stuck his unshaved face out, and squinted at the sun. His sandy hair was uncombed, and his unsmiling face showed no trace of his usual breezy disposition.

"Morning," Scott said cheerfully. "Big party last night?"

Davey lit a cigarette. "More like a fuckin' wake."

"Sorry about the shutdown," Scott said.

Davey had no interest in conversation and looked off at the water, much as Vic had a few moments earlier, smoking and staring glumly into space. Slowly, the other fishermen began to show signs of life, not with the usual shouting and kidding around, but with a lot of bitching and long faces. Everyone was taking the shutdown hard, which only pointed more clearly to their mounting financial troubles. It was, Scott thought, catching some of the mood himself, not a fair world.

Further evidence the men were getting beat down was the lack of care they were taking with their boats. Even on the *Nellie J* there were bottles, boots, fishing tackle, cans, and plastic buckets cluttering up the deck, and the whole ship looked in need of a hosing down. Normally, Vic ran one of the sharpest boats around, and, for all that, Vic, Davey, and the others were also happy men by nature. Scott found it depressing.

Vic leaned over the port rail to lower a crab pot into the water.

"Where's the rest of your crew, Vic?"

"They took off."

"Don't see the *Olga* anywhere."

"She's up on the block."

"You're selling her?" This was a new revelation and something of a surprise, since Vic had a deep attachment to the boat.

Vic shrugged. "Who needs two boats?"

Scott knew there was another reason. In the good years, Vic ran three boats—the *Nellie J*, named after his first wife, the *Olga C*, named after his second, and the *Brunhilde*, which, following the last divorce, he'd named after his since-departed German shepherd. Vic's son Mark had skippered the *Brunhilde*, but when Mark returned to college at the end of the season, Vic sold the ship because, as he told Scott, two boats were enough. Now, apparently, one was to be enough.

As was their usual routine, Georgie started the lift that unrolled the net from the reel and spilled it over the boom. They let it roll until yards of loose pieces of net drifted onto the dock. Here it would dry while they repaired the tears from their last catch. As Vic said, he wanted it ready when the "fuckin' bureaucrats" decided to let them out again.

"I'll help," Scott said.

"There's some waders in the cabin."

Scott fetched the waders and pulled them on over his jeans, and they all went at it, rolling out the net while water sloshed under their boots. For the next hour they worked tying string to broken sections of mesh and spreading the coarse fabric out on the deck to dry. Doing something, even this monotonous task, gave one a sense of purpose.

Vic's spirits picked up. He became chatty, teasing Georgie and showing more than a bystander's interest in Owen's murder. "I heard you got called in on it, Doc."

Scott nodded. "Too late, though. He'd been dead a couple hours. Had a hole in his middle the size of a baseball."

"Gawd." Georgie whistled.

"Had to get pretty damn close to do that kind of damage, even with a shotgun," Vic observed as he cinched up a loose end of mesh. "I remember a lieutenant in Korea, took an M16 in the chest. Split him open like a can of spaghetti. Poor bastard didn't know what hit him."

Georgie stopped working, removed the waders, and dangled his bare feet over the stern. "Wouldn't you think Owen would've beat it out of there? I mean, hey, if somebody pointed a double-gauge at me, I'd split so fast all they'd see of me would be my butt."

Interested in Georgie's observations, Scott said, "As a matter of fact, he didn't look like he'd run a step. Must've froze. Fear will do that."

Vic disagreed. "Didn't expect to get shot."

"You think it was someone he knew and trusted?"

"Why not? Everybody who knew him hated his guts."

"Add to that, his house is impossible to see from the road."

"Not from the water," Georgie said, catching Vic's frown.

"We see those flaky friends of his flitting 'round there, boozing it up every weekend."

"You were out that day, weren't you, Vic?" Scott said.

"Wasn't anywhere near the place."

After a time they quit work to sit on the deck in the shade of the skiff. The conversation worked its way back to Owen. Georgie, who'd given much thought to the murder, had his own suspicions.

"Do you have anyone particular in mind?"

Georgie folded up his long legs Indian-style and leaned forward confidentially. "I'd take a hard look at Bob Delaney."

Scott was surprised at the second mention of the real estate man.

"Or that wired-up wife of his."

"Marilyn?"

"Yeah, the foxy blonde who whips in and out of here in the Tollycraft."

Scott had a mental picture of Marilyn Delaney aiming her Tolly at Griffin Bay and shooting out of the creek like a rocket on a sled. The commission had warned her more than once about breaking the five-knot speed limit for the creek. Scott also remembered Toni had never liked Marilyn, and that Al thought her sadly lacking in gray cells. To this point, Scott disagreed. Marilyn was bright enough, but was the type who thought empty-headedness won male approval.

"'Course, she's not the only dame jets outta here, but you can tell when it's her 'cause she's always talking. Voices carry real good on the water, and you can hear her all the way to Seal Rock, going on about those parties of Owen's."

"Anything in particular about them?"

"Well, the drinking, and the wheeling and dealing . . . lotta that, and stocks, condo deals, and the like."

"Were Delaney's involved?"

"Up to their necks. According to Marilyn, Wentworth screwed them real good on one deal."

"Which one was that?"

Georgie shrugged, apparently bored with details. "I dunno. She was talking to the mousy-looking lady who runs a Bayliner. I think she said something about a land deal in Gold River, or maybe it was Campbell River." He thought a moment. "Anyways, somewhere on Vancouver Island."

In all of what Georgie said, nothing incriminated Delaney any more than the other victims of Owen's sharp dealings. It proved what Scott already knew—that Owen had been a cheat— and left Scott with the same gnawing questions. Why had Toni had anything to do with a man like Owen? And, for that matter, why had Vic invested in West Coast?

They went back to mending the nets. Without a breeze of any kind, the creek soon heated up like an oven. Scott took off the waders and stripped to his shorts. Dandy crawled under the skiff, rolled over on his back, and fell asleep, snoring loudly. The sun put a glare on the water, so Scott had to squint. The masts of a big ketch flashed white as it started out of Griffin Bay in front of the sun. It was under power and fell in behind a line of pleasure cruisers heading north up San Juan Channel.

After a while they stopped working and sat around, drinking beer, while Vic told stories about his Alaska runs, about ships colliding and disappearing in the fog. "You never saw anything like it. The *Anna Marie* went right off my radar, never saw her again."

"Were you running heavy seas?"

Something of a mystic in many ways, Vic rolled his brown eyes and talked about mysterious forces. "No storms. Nothin' like that. Mark said it had to do with magnetic pulls. Carl said there were big undertows on the Inside Passage. All I know is we never saw her again, not a trace, and all hands were lost."

Scott had heard the story a number of times, each time told with a different twist, and whether true or a figment of Vic's imagination, Scott had never been sure.

"I hear you picked up a nice load of sockeye in the trap this week." The trap was a deep tidal pool about four hundred yards off South Beach where the experienced fishermen often found good runs of salmon. It was a relatively small spot, which the older men, like Vic, considered their private reserve. Too late, Scott caught the eye signals from Georgie, whose face screwed up as though he'd bit into a lemon.

Curses rolled off Vic's lips. It was an incident involving Vic's boat and the Indians. The *Nellie J* had started her set off South Beach, and one of the Indian boats, a bow picker, moved in and crowded her. Vic's face darkened. "Laid his net right into the pocket just as Georgie started the swing. I fixed him. I cranked the wheel, turned into his net, and the son of a bitch crossed his own net beating it out of there."

"They left hoppin' mad," Georgie agreed. "We nearly ran over them. Almost lost our own net in the bargain."

"They won't be back," Vic said, ignoring the disapproval in Georgie's voice. "If they come 'round again, I'll blow their fuckin' canoe right out of the water."

"But you got a good price for the sockeye?" The question, intended to defuse his friend's anger, only stoked the fire.

"Hell no! The new buyer's stealing us blind."

Georgie explained: "This is the same bunch that put West Coast on the skids. Outbid them until West Coast ran outta dough and chased all the small buyers out."

It was familiar enough. The new buyer was now all there was, and the fishermen had to take whatever price was offered. No wonder Vic had put money into West Coast. It was a move of desperation. What else might a desperate man do?

Eight

The following day, Scott decided to get the engine on the *Picaroon* in top working condition. He'd promised Erin a sail, and weather reports forecast moderate winds. He was bent over the engine well, changing the oil on the Grey, when he heard the sound of heels on the dock. It was Marilyn Delaney, decked out in snow-white slacks, a bright red sun top, and open-toed sandals. She clicked right over, leaned over the well, and smiled tobacco and perfume all over him.

"Scott," she said. "Thought it was you. Lorene said you were on the island. Where you been hiding yourself?"

Scott wiped grease off his hands with a rag and looked up into canary-blond hair and an evenly tanned face. "A looker," Georgie called her. She was that, by any standards.

He smiled up at her. "Where you off to?"

"I'm meeting Bob at Roche. He's taking some clients out for a spin."

"How *is* Bob?"

She lifted her arms in disgust. "All wrapped up in real estate. Sales, sales, sales! We're running these people over to Sidney for lunch today, the mainland tomorrow. Bob uses the boat for business so he can take it off his taxes, which is all right if you don't mind who you associate with. For my part, I like to pick my friends, if you know what I mean."

Georgie hadn't exaggerated about Marilyn. "Wired," Georgie said.

"Next week it's Campbell River again, and that's how it goes.

Hard to catch ourselves coming and going. Never see anyone on the Cape anymore." Except Owen. She'd seen him the night he died. "Terrible, wasn't it?" She hugged her long brown arms. "I shiver thinking about it. Getting so a person isn't safe anywhere."

"Hard to think of a killer among one's neighbors," Scott said.

It wasn't what she had in mind. "You don't honestly think someone on our Cape shot Owen? It was the motorcyclists, I'm just sure of it, the way they tear around the lighthouse, all doped up. Bob says they'd do anything for money to buy their drugs. You heard they stole one of Owen's African masks? Owen told me once how much they cost. Would you believe we could buy a brand-new thirty-foot Tolly for the price of just one of those creepy things? I told Owen he should keep them under lock and key. He'd be alive today if he had. Makes you sick, doesn't it?"

She continued talking long after her mind ran out of thoughts, then, looking at her watch, said, "Damn! Bob will be chewing nails." With a little toss of her head, she started for the twenty-six-foot Tollycraft tied to the outside slip.

"Won't take you long in that job," Scott said, looking at the inboard-outboard that powered her. "What have you there? Couple hundred horses?"

She smiled. "Three hundred. Marvelous, isn't it? Bob says I get carried away when I get behind the wheel, but I love going fast, letting the spray hit my face. Gives me a feeling of power, you know what I mean?"

Scott laughed. "I'm a sailor, remember?"

"You don't know what you're missing. When you want to try it, let me know. It's exhilarating, I can tell you."

She climbed the ladder to her flying bridge and turned on the big engine. With surprising skill, she backed the boat out of its slip, paused briefly to wave, then, as Georgie had described, rocketed out of the creek, her hair blowing like straw in the wind. The Tolly kicked up a wake that would have swamped a tug.

Scott was just finishing with the Grey when Erin arrived. "A perfect day," she said, breathing deeply of the air.

"Fair wind," he agreed.

A ripple started across the creek. The forecasts called for freshening late in the afternoon, but it was still only eleven, which gave them plenty of time for a good run before any problems might develop.

They started out with a gentle wind at their backs, bright sun, and no cloud cover. Scott set a course up San Juan Channel to Upright Head, and the jib billowed out like a plumped-up pillow, leading the way. The only sound was the soft rush of water against the hull and the rustle of Dacron filling in the wind. Two seagulls on a log floated past. Erin saluted them. They looked back, uninterested.

"You won't feel we're going fast with the wind behind us, but we're actually running close to four knots, which isn't bad," Scott said.

Erin's only previous experience had been with the little C-Larks on the lake. This was totally different.

He steered toward Shaw Island. They spoke infrequently, and Erin seemed not the least uncomfortable with the silence. She was content to watch, learn by observing, and do, without asking pointless questions. She was a good sailor and good company.

Beyond Turn Rock, the wind shifted. There was a little bite to it now. It stung the cheeks and moistened the eyes. Erin took the helm and quickly had the *Picaroon* heeled so water spilled lightly over the gunwales and trickled along the decks. A flotilla of pleasure cruisers coming from Upright Head overtook them, rumbled past, stirring big rolls of water that broke over the *Picaroon*'s bow. Water gushed and tumbled into a cascade of spray that traveled the length of the deck and showered them both. It ran off Scott's jacket and puddled up in the cockpit, where Erin stood in a pool of water. Erin pushed dripping strands of pale hair back from her face and put on a jacket. They headed into Friday Harbor, and a small ketch moved up swiftly behind them.

"Should I fall off the wind?"

"Keep your course. He'll pass on our starboard."

She watched the ketch doubtfully. It was a race. The boy piloting the ketch was enjoying the contest, running a little recklessly with sails trimmed taut, gaining on them, crowding. Another string of cruisers increased the chop, and the *Picaroon* bobbed and pitched. The ketch moved up, ran so close they heard her sails whipping and snapping in the wind. She closed the gap to a whisker. Erin's eyes fastened on the threadlike path of water that separated the two boats.

"Should we come about?"

"Just hold her steady."

The ketch had more square footage of sail, which gave her the edge. A fresh burst of wind drove her forward. In one quick surge, she winged by, jib trimmed to the wind, sails working in concert, passed with only the flash of a whitecap and the whipping of sails between them. Her skipper waved a victory salute, and Scott was so close he could have counted every button on his shirt. Erin waved back, her face flushed with energy. "She handles beautifully, Scott."

It was just past noon when they drew near the breakwater in Friday Harbor. They handed down the sails and motored in. Friday was its usual mangle of boaters and tourists. They tied up at the guest float and hiked to the top of the hill and a small café that overlooked the customs dock. It was a particularly pleasant spot, and the restaurant quickly filled with more boaters.

"Grandpa says you're up for the whole summer," Erin said conversationally.

"Didn't he tell you I've more or less moved to the islands permanently?"

She seemed surprised. "You left your practice?"

"Yes."

"What a shame. Everyone says you're such a wonderful surgeon."

He sipped a glass of Chardonnay and waited for the next assault, the one Al constantly harped on, about his training and the rest of it. It never came. She started talking about the sail.

At the patio's edge, the flag on the pole snapped like a

starched shirt on a line. More boats coming in. None going out. The waitress brought coffee and dessert, and Erin talked about Victoria, Vancouver Island's largest city, "a little bit of old England," and only an hour's run by fast boat from the Cape.

"Funny about the African mask turning up in Victoria," she said. And then, "Did I tell you Leroy called yesterday? He wanted to see if we had overlooked anything. Oh, that reminds me. I ran into a friend of yours yesterday. Preston Fields."

The second time Fields had come up in the past few days. "How do you happen to know Pres?"

"I met him when he stopped in to see Grandpa."

"I didn't know he and Al were friends."

"I don't think they are. Preston wanted Grandpa to serve on the committee to save the whales. Actually, what Preston wanted was the use of Grandpa's name, to give the group prestige."

"Did Al join?"

"No. He wants the whales to have the protection of law and all that. He says it's that he doesn't trust Preston."

"And you, what do you think of Preston?" His mind was on Toni at Owen's party with the marine biologist, and the sarcasm slipped into his voice.

She picked it up. "He's intelligent, sensitive. Did you know he organized an athletic workshop for the high school kids on the island?"

No, he hadn't known. Scott attacked the rest of his pie.

They finished lunch and headed out of the harbor in gusting winds, with sails up and Scott at the helm. A cloud speared the southern sky, and the water took on broad patches of gray. The wind blew the spray against his face, and he tasted salt. Ought to have warned him. Suddenly there were no boats coming or going through the passageways. Only the wind kicked up the chop. Coming around Brown Island, Scott's windometer registered twenty knots. No problem, but a look at the fast-disappearing sun told him the wind might build. He looked at his watch. Only one-thirty. Should he go back to Friday or run it out?

Unaware of his concern, Erin began talking about how she'd

always wanted to sail in a good wind with a skipper who knew his stuff, or something equally silly. The wind let out a howl and blew his jacket full. Across the bay the waters churned up. They were only an hour's run to the creek, and Scott had, after all, sailed in much heavier winds. It wasn't particularly enjoyable, and required concentration and hard work. But he'd done it many times, usually alone. "We'll run for it," he said.

He studied the peaks of the waves as the rolls tumbled and toppled into foam. They were breaking at a height of three to four feet. He could handle it. But in the distance the waves appeared to rise and fall more sharply. Could get rougher as they started into more open waters.

Erin sensed his indecision. "Should we have left earlier?"

"No problem. A bit more wind than we had coming up. We'll reef down, give less sail to the wind. Makes for a smoother ride, even if it takes us a few minutes longer. I think it would be a good idea to slip on the life jackets, though."

Erin went below to retrieve them, handed Scott one, and put hers on. Over the heavy outer clothing the jacket made for a lot of bulk, and she made a joke about it as she struggled to make it fit. The wind whistled through the open hatch.

Scott considered taking the inside passage around Turn Island, but decided against it. Maneuvering the shoal pass in bad weather could be difficult under sail. He ran the main down until it looked like a crib-size sheet, and steered a course the long way around Turn. The *Picaroon* quickly settled in. The action was mostly up and down, not too uncomfortable. But when they rounded the buoy off Turn Rock, everything changed. The boat started to roll. With the water moving in so many different directions it was hard to keep her pointed. Big whirling rollers lifted her up out of the water and dropped her back. She swayed and heaved. It was miserably uncomfortable now, with the waves striking from all sides. Erin had to hold on to the cockpit rail to keep from falling.

"Always get a rip in here," Scott said, trying to reassure her.

The windometer edged over thirty knots, and the increased noise made hearing difficult. He had to shout to be heard. "We've been overpowered. We'll go on the reach, let out the main, take some of the pressure off."

It meant a change of direction. If she was frightened of changing direction in these heavy seas, she gave no sign of it. She understood about turning from her experience in the C-Larks. She knew about letting the bow swing into the wind, allowing the jib to flutter free while the boat took its new heading. There was only one potential problem.

"We need enough momentum to swing the hull around," Scott explained. "The cross chop tends to slow our forward motion, which means we have to cinch the jib down quickly so we don't lose the wind and wallow in the waves." He didn't add that if they lost their forward progress in these swirling seas, they could go over too far. Boats sometimes heeled far enough to capsize when coming about in a storm, and it was this possibility he was thinking about as he prepared to start their turn. "Ready to come about?"

She nodded, and watched for his signal.

"Hard alee!" He cranked the wheel. The *Picaroon* started to turn. The jib fluttered loose as Erin let go the sheets that held the boat. Waves piled up on all sides. Water smashed into the bow, let loose over the cabin, and spilled into the well. Erin worked frantically to secure the lines. Scott helped her winch in. The *Picaroon* started over on her side, leaned so far her gunwales brushed the cresting waves. She gained speed, started back up, and stretched out in her new direction. Scott eased the main sheet to unleash the boom, and played out the big sail. She bulged like a parachute. The rocking motion subsided. The boat gained speed, started back up, and stretched out on her new tack.

"Well done!" Scott said.

But across the cockpit, Erin, her eyes on the water behind them, did not look pleased. Scott soon saw the cause, a small Whaler coming out of the passage by Turn Island, tracking a bumpy path toward the channel.

"Who would be crazy enough to take a runabout out in this?" she asked.

"Don't worry. He'll head back as soon as he sees what it's like out here."

The weather worsened. Their jackets blew puffy sleeves, and the water splashed their faces so much that seeing was a problem. Gale-force winds are defined as thirty-five knots or more, and, according to Scott's instruments, some of these gusts were blowing in excess of forty. These were the kind of winds that demasted ships, the kind of winds that could pick a small boat out of the chop, flip her upside down, and throw her back, head-down into the sea. Scott looked back, strained to see through the gushing stream that flew through the rigging. Twisting and turning, the Whaler cleared the pass and pressed on. Must be kids, Scott decided.

The opposing forces of the incoming tides formed cavernous foaming eddies, and the *Picaroon* began to pitch, climbing up one wave, crashing down another. The boat caught one on her side and rolled. It was more uncomfortable than dangerous, but it took all Scott's attention to keep her head up, and he started to think about bringing the main down farther. Motoring without his sail would be worse, he decided. The *Picaroon* had been converted from a lifeboat hull, and hadn't much ballast. She'd roll even more without the sail to stabilize her. There was uncertainty in Erin's face.

"It's always the worst out here in the open," Scott shouted. "Won't be long. We're moving well."

Erin nodded. By now she knew the dangers that still faced them. Scott fixed a bearing on Seal Rock across Griffin Bay. A few more minutes to the creek.

"Scott, the little boat, it's still coming."

The Whaler was fighting its way toward them, two people aboard. It slammed over the whirlpools, motor in and out of the waves, planed and dipped, spouting water over her bow like one of the killer whales, and, like the whales, came up for air and kept going.

62

The long cloud that had started like a sword across the horizon lengthened. All at once the entire sky was filled with it. The Whaler continued to beat a choppy and determined path directly behind them.

"Are they racing us? They couldn't be that stupid, could they?" Erin asked.

"If they aren't careful, they'll get themselves broached." And fall overboard, and, Scott thought irritably, we'll have to risk our necks pulling them out. Who were these fools who'd come out in gale-force winds in a small outboard? Then he remembered that he was a fool who'd come out in it, too.

The Whaler gained on them. A hundred yards off Pear Point, Erin made an observation. The two men aboard the Whaler, the ones called Charlie and Jerry, were the same two who'd come into the café on Friday. They'd ordered a beer, she said, and started to leave without paying, and the waitress had called them back. The incident had gone by Scott completely.

It had been an insane idea until now. Scott hadn't seen their faces that night. Now, as he strained to see across the short fetch of water, he still couldn't make them out clearly, but he remembered the heavy shoulders on Charlie, the driver, and the long arms of his companion, arms that swung a club like a baseball bat. It couldn't possibly be coincidence.

All that separated the Whaler from them now was the unpredictable breaking of the waves, which impeded the Whaler's forward motion. Who were these men? What was their purpose out here in the nearly empty seas? Scott already had an answer. It was crazy, dangerous; but these weren't careful men. They'd taken the sheltered passage out of Friday, hoped, staying close to shore, to catch the *Picaroon*, unprotected, alone, force her into a broach, capsize her, and return safely to Friday the same way they came. To be capsized wasn't necessarily the worst of it. Going over with sails furled, chances are air would be trapped under the boat, and she wouldn't sink right away. But these waters were cold, less than forty degrees even in the heat of summer. When a plane crashed in the sound sometime back,

Scott remembered, people had died of hypothermia in less than fifteen minutes. What a stupid mess he'd gotten them into.

He weighed his alternatives. He could lift the main and get their speed up and quite possibly be demasted or risk tearing the sails to shreds, or he could wait for the Whaler to play a game of chicken in which the *Picaroon* would veer to avoid being cut in two and be broached. There appeared no choice at all.

The *Picaroon* dropped into a trough. Water flooded the cockpit. It was an effort just to hold on to the wheel against the power of the wind and the sea. For the first time, fear showed itself on Erin's face.

"They're going to hit us."

Scott shook his head. That wasn't the idea. Even if they rammed the *Picaroon* and managed to drive a hole big enough to sink her, the impact would most likely upend the Whaler as well. It was a matter of angles and forces of the waves. Maybe these two could do it, get out unscathed, but Scott doubted it very much.

"You think they're playing a game?" Erin's voice edged up.

He didn't tell her what he actually thought, that they wanted to force the *Picaroon* to turn abruptly, which would send the boat over in six-foot swells, then, if need be, put a line on her and finish the job. The *Picaroon* couldn't outrun the Whaler even in this chop, even if they ran with full sail, which was, at this point, unthinkable. If he came about too swiftly he would most likely accomplish what they were after, anyway, and possibly get struck midships in the bargain. Whoever these two were, they knew ships and were familiar with these waters.

Erin had a desperate look in her eyes as she held on to the cockpit rail, her hair blowing wildly in the wind. There was no time left in the test of wills. The pilot of the Whaler took a bounce and opened her up. In speed, the *Picaroon* was no match for the double-hulled speedboat. Scott remembered thinking, *We'll go over, be thrown into the sea, left to drown.* An eight-foot roller broke over their stern. The Whaler hurtled over it. Scott had no time to prepare Erin. He pulled in the main. "Ready to jibe!" He was counting on her experience with those C-Larks.

Erin flew across the cockpit to the lines.

"Jibe!" A turn *away* from the wind, not into it, to gather speed, not lose it, a racing turn, with danger of demasting in heavy winds.

The Whaler's bow nosed up. The *Picaroon* swung 'round. Scott watched the mast with a tight chest as he thought: Have to warn Erin to stay away from the main, find the high place, hang on. The sloop pulled and twisted, gaining speed. Another roller crashed over the bow. The *Picaroon* nosed up, aimed at the Whaler's belly.

The pilot of the Whaler had a look of panic as he laid on the wheel. For one breathless count of five he spun, around and around in a dizzy circle. Erin's scream died on the wind as the Whaler skipped loose and pounded over the waves, up and down and sideways, out of control. It flew across the reef, ran up the pumice-scarred beach at Pear Point, and, scraping and cracking, piled up on the rocks.

Nine

"I don't believe it," Erin said in a voice close to breaking. "They made it!"

The two crawled out of the Whaler, and, on hands and feet like crabs, scrambled across the beach. Too damn easy, Scott thought. If they'd been tossed into the ice-cold sound and left to drown, it would have been no more than they deserved.

No time for a second look. The wind had increased. It whiffled and moaned through the rigging, rattled around the cabin, and blew in Scott's face, bringing with it fresh spurts of frothing spray. The waves twisted around them wildly, slamming against the sides of the hull and throwing water over the decks and into the well faster than the scuppers could handle it. Below decks the pots that had fallen off the stove banged against the toeboards, a mild annoyance in the midst of their other troubles, but a reminder they weren't out of danger yet. Ahead was Griffin Bay, but between the bay and the creek were three miles of open, thundering sea.

"If only the wind would let up," Erin said dispiritedly, pushing back thick strands of wet hair that blew into her eyes and dripped water on her cheeks.

Scott pointed to Mount Finlayson's hump rising over the Cape and tried to force lightness into his voice. "We'll be protected once we get inside the lee of the land. We'll have to come about once more, but then it's a straight shot to the creek."

She smiled feebly. Clearly the clash with the Whaler had weakened her nerve. He knew what she was thinking: another turn into the wind, another chance at being broached. They hadn't much choice.

"Ready?"

She nodded and waited, hand poised on the cleat.

Scott turned into the flurry of two crossing waves. It was like riding a chute. Water piled up all around. The bow went up, and the whole deck slid out from under them. Water rushed over the side onto the decks in a flood, and they started to roll like a canoe. The ballast wasn't heavy enough to counter the forces of wind and sea, and she started over. The boat creaked and groaned and kept right on going. If the main touches the water, Scott thought with a sickening sense of helplessness, we've had it.

He thought about the *Anna Marie* coming down from Alaska on the Inside Passage, running alongside Vic when she was pulled into the undertow. Scott stared into the giant ring of swirling waters and felt the *Picaroon* continue to slip. He could feel his heart pound. He was breathing in spurts, his air choked off by the realization they might be sucked into a black hole a hundred fathoms deep.

Erin braced her feet against the bulkhead, her eyes fixed on the mast. "We're going over!"

Her faint voice, like a whisper over the wind, trumpeted in Scott's ears. "No, we're not!"

He eased the line, played it out until she started to luff and whip free in the wind. Another roller hammered the bow, and it looked as though they'd be swamped in a final tug-of-war between the crossworking breakers, dragged under like the *Anna Marie*, "disappearing without a trace."

"No, dammit," Scott said again, this time to himself. He let the sails go completely free. Dacron flapped violently in the wind, and he feared the sails might rip right up their seams.

Almost in response to his voice, with the pressure off the mast, the *Picaroon* stopped her horizontal descent. She wavered a moment, undecided, and then, water sloshing the decks, inched back up. The struggle to remain upright turned into an up-and-down action as the *Picaroon* ploughed around in the enormous whirls of water.

Scott and Erin hauled the main in until it resembled a shrunken pillowslip, and he started up the Grey. Under power and sail, the *Picaroon* resumed a pitching and yawing course straight for the creek. The waves continued to build in front of them. They started down, dropped four feet into a hole, scaled back up. There were more of these, heart-stopping drops, breath-holding climbs. Scott had to catch them head-on, had to roll gently with the chop, there being no margin for miscalculation. Not much farther to go, almost out of the cross chop. All he had to do was keep her headed. A plunging wave curled and broke into foam over the bow. They shot across the crest of the next swell. They were closing in on the shore's shelf. The jetty rose to their port.

Scott shouted encouragement. "We're almost in the lee of the point."

Another wave spilled over the bow, and water trickled down the deck. Another followed, putting up only a fine spray. Definitely easing. Ahead was Fish Creek and Mount Finlayson acting like a giant breaker on the wind. The creek opened up its protective arms in front of them, and the *Picaroon* settled to a gentle rock. The rollers turned into slop, and Scott steered a course past Seal Rock, into the creek, bounced over a wavelet, and turned past the gill-netters rafted along the north dock. He wanted to send up a cheer, but there was no one aboard the fishing boats to hear. He turned easily into the slip, and with Erin secured the boat to her cleats.

Scott let out a long, gratifying sigh and grinned across the cockpit. He hugged Erin, and she hugged him back in joyful relief. "You were great," he said. "Just great."

There was concern on Al's face as they walked through the doorway, the wind ushering them in with a howl. "Been watching those waves for the past half hour. Pretty wild out there."

Erin kissed his cheek and began to jabber as people do after a release of great tension. "No need to worry. Scott can manage anything." She heaped praise on him, saying nothing about the obvious, that he'd used abominably bad judgment getting them in the fix in the first place.

"You should have seen your granddaughter," Scott said. "Hauled those sails like a pro." He reached for the telephone, then paused to breathe in the aroma of brandy from the glass Al handed him. "Isn't this your Christmas stuff?"

The old man shrugged, and his thin face lit up in a smile. "You're both back safe and sound."

Scott called Leroy. He was out, according to the dispatcher. This was urgent, Scott explained. She said she'd try to find him, and rang off.

Erin settled in front of the fire and began drying her hair. The phone rang.

It was Leroy, and he was at Roche Harbor, on the other side of the island, a good thirty-minute drive from Friday Harbor. Scott poured out the story. Could Leroy send his deputies right over to Pear Point? "Better check out the airport and the ferry landing, too. You might want to call ahead to Anacortes. They might've caught the three-thirty ferry."

Leroy groaned on the other end, and Scott figured he resented the advice. "Sorry," Scott said, "but they've had a good head start. I thought you'd want to get right on it."

"Wouldn't do any good. Can't touch them without a warrant or a positive ID."

"I'll come right in."

"Not necessary."

"If we don't do something, they'll be gone."

"Relax, Doc. I'll call you as soon as I turn up something."

Scott put the phone down with a dissatisfied sigh and faced the questioning faces of Erin and Al.

Al frowned. "Apparently you had more of an afternoon than I thought."

"What's all this about a break-in?" Erin said with accusing eyes for both of them. Al explained, and Erin looked at Scott, bewildered. "But what were they after?"

"I haven't a clue."

"You didn't tell me you'd seen them before."

"But I never really *saw* them. Not their faces, anyway."

"Then how do you know it's the same two?"

"They move the same, the boat's the same." They were familiar in other ways, but he wasn't sure why.

Outside, the wind let out a quick burst that rattled the windows. Al checked the firepit for a downdraft, but the flames rose steadily up the stack.

"You think those men killed Owen, right?" Erin said. "And now they're after you."

"Doesn't add up," Al said. "If they'd wanted to kill Scottie, they would have shot him on the beach when they had the chance."

"But they were after him today. I was there. And I think they'll try again."

Scott shook his head in disagreement. "I think the sheriff has it right there. It was undoubtedly an idea they dreamed up on the spur of the moment. When it didn't work, they took off. The only question is what they were after when they broke into my house."

Erin wasn't persuaded. "If it's tied into Owen, as you both seem to think, why would they be after anything at your house?"

Looking a little less upset, Al said, "Maybe it has something to do with Scott examining Owen."

Erin thought that over and rejected it.

They were still puzzling it when Leroy called again. "No trace of them," he said. "But we found the Whaler piled up on the beach at Pear Point, just like you said." According to Leroy, it belonged to one of the university people at the experimental lab who'd reported it stolen three days before. "Thanks for putting us on to it, Doc. 'Course, it's a total washout. Cracks in the glass, and the motor's bent all to hell." They would, he said, keep looking for the two men. "It's a little like picking needles out of haystacks until we get a better description."

"I told you we'd come in."

"No hurry. Tomorrow morning will do. We've covered every

corner of town. Let's face it, they aren't going to show their faces on the streets tonight." Clearly, he didn't see a tie-in to Owen, and catching them wasn't among his highest priorities. "This island might surprise you. We get break-ins all the time, and it's damn seldom we find the ones who did it."

"But they didn't take anything."

"They probably wanted to shake you up a little, get even for the fight on the beach. We see it all the time."

Scott agreed to see the sheriff in the morning, then put the phone down in disgust. Erin was certain Leroy had misunderstood. "He understood, all right. The way he sees it, we're still among the living, and the *Picaroon* is none the worse for wear." Scott shrugged. "For anyone who wasn't there it sounds farfetched suggesting they tried to kill us."

By the window, Al had been silent. "I see they gave the fishermen a night out." He pointed to the procession of gillnetters bouncing through Cattle Pass.

"What a tough way to make a living," Erin said. "Going out in this awful stuff."

Scott nodded. Vic wouldn't be out tonight. The purse seiners had the daytime run, but the smaller boats, the gillnetters, would be out there, working their nets with a wall of water coming at them.

Scott's gaze fixed on Davey Olson's bow picker, the *Mollie O*, as she took the passage in front of Goose Island at full throttle, skillfully avoiding the rock outcropping hidden by the high tide. The *Mollie O* was small, her cabin aft, her reel midships, a planing boat with plenty of speed. That's what Davey counted on to keep him out of trouble. Of course, for him, as for all the boats, there were always those nights when the motor would go, and they'd sit it out, rocking around in a black pit until another gillnetter might happen by to give a tow, and both boats would be out their catch for the night. Scott had always admired the fishermen their toughness, their peculiar mix of fatalism and mulish will.

"They go out in everything," he said.

Ten

The sky, like the water, was dark and unfriendly as Scott and Dandy walked against the bracing chill of the wind across the road to his cabin. Late, and getting to be a habit, Scott thought pleasantly. It had been a day full to the limit. Caught in a gale, nearly run down, almost broached, and, strangely, looking back on it, he'd enjoyed himself more than he had in months.

He switched on the lights in the living room, and Dandy went for his dish and the remains of his morning kibble. The dog's crunching and the wind rushing through the eaves were the only sounds in the house. Scott snapped on his shortwave and dropped into the big chair. One of his favorite pastimes on the lonely nights was to listen to the fishermen chattering on their radios. Sometimes the calls were important, a boat in trouble, a net hooked by another boat that could wipe out an entire season's profits. Mostly, however, the calls were just talk to fill a long night.

The voice from the marine weather station in Victoria droned monotonously: ". . . high pressure ridge building on the coast . . . Cape Mudge, gale- to storm-force southerlies . . . Strait of Juan de Fuca, gale-force winds, gusting to forty knots . . ."

Scott switched channels. The voices of the fishermen bleated in and out, about as usual.

"Got a full load, Ray. I'm heading into Friday."

"Lucky son of a bitch."

Another voice: "Whatcha pickin' up, Todd?"

"Nothing but fuckin' green-eyes. They're tearing hell outta my nets."

The talk went on. Finally Scott looked at the clock. Time to close up shop. He reached to turn off the set. It was exactly five minutes after one. Davey Olson's baritone voice broke into the channel, sounding like a second tenor. "This is the *Mollie O* calling the Coast Guard. Come in, Coast Guard." Davey repeated the call and, receiving no reply, repeated again, this time frantically, "Where the hell are you, Coast Guard?"

Scott started for the phone, and a voice, slow and calm, answered Davey. "This is the Coast Guard cutter 00539. What's the trouble, *Mollie O?*"

"I picked up a body in my net. White male, I think. What in hell do I do with it?"

"What's your location?"

It was off South Beach. Scott grabbed his car keys and his jacket and started out the door, Dandy on his heels. The Coast Guard was still talking. "Keep your heading, *Mollie O*. We should pick you up in twenty minutes."

The wind buffeted the Jeep so much that the vehicle swung across the center stripe as Scott took the curve by the lighthouse at a good clip. The sky was black, but over the water the bouncing lights from the gill-netters blinked like stars. Beyond the sand dunes the road straightened, and he laid a heavier foot on the accelerator. Dandy lost his balance and slid into Scott's lap. Scott eased up on the pedal.

He was thinking about that body in Davey's net and the two men and remembering why they'd been familiar. Had the *Mollie O* dragged up a victim from a skirmish on the decks of the *Pilgrim* four nights ago? Were the men on the Whaler the same ones who'd worked the lines on the schooner's afterdeck? Had those two clubbed a man to death in the fog that night, or was it only Scott's nightmare revisited?

Scott braked the Jeep against a stack of driftwood, and, fighting violent gusts of wind, he and Dandy started climbing over the logs that littered the path to the water's edge. Big waves lifted logs out of their sand and rock beds and rolled them back into the sea.

They'd be transferring the body to the Coast Guard cutter not far from here. Big plunging breakers thundered over the beach, sending off a phosphorescent glow that lit up the sand.

The wind was sharp. Scott turned up his jacket collar and plodded closer to the stretch of sea where the fishing boats were at work. He picked a spot where the sand and rocks converged and stood there, listening for the rumble of diesels over the howling wind. All across the water in front of South Beach the gill-netters stretched out end to end, bobbing like corks. Somewhere among them was the *Mollie O*, waiting, half her net dragging against the tide and the chop, with a crab-picked body snarled in the other half.

Out over the strait, like a well-choreographed ballet, the little boats forged a path between their nets for the Coast Guard to slip through. Flashing signals lit up the center of their ring, and these, Scott guessed, came from the *Mollie O*'s lamps.

Time passed slowly on the darkened beach. The roar of wind and tide blotted out the voices that he could have heard on a calm night, the cursing and bitching at the delay that was costing the men a set, at the frustration of Davey and his crew as they cut up their net, separating fish and seaweed to unload their unwanted cargo.

Strong floods lit up the channel around Cattle Point, signaling the arrival of the Coast Guard. Scott imagined he heard the cheers of relief from all the boats, the loudest aboard the *Mollie O*. The cutter steamed through the path provided by the gill-netters, and the transfer began. It would be no fun on a night like this, with the water pounding their hulls, boats tossing and banging against each other, scraping paint and jarring nerves. From the beach, Scott waited. After what seemed hours, but in actuality was less than thirty minutes, the cutter started to back up and swing out as it headed for Friday Harbor.

Scott started for the Jeep, anxious now to see what Davey had dragged up from the bottom of the trap.

In Friday Harbor a crowd collected around the customs dock as Scott parked the Jeep. For a town already reeling from one murder, Scott imagined this latest would have everyone stirred up. The docks were well lit from the Coast Guard floods, so it looked like a Seahawk game on a Saturday night in the Dome. "You stay here, boy," Scott told Dandy, and he walked down the ramp toward the lights.

The sheriff's staff was doing its level best to deal with the latest crisis, but it was much more than they were used to, considering a normal day's log consisted of complaints about barking dogs and domestic arguments. Leroy's deputy, Harold Cane, stood beside the sheriff's patrol car, blocking entrance to the dock. He grinned when he saw Scott.

"Leroy will be glad to see you. One of the gill-netters dragged up a corpse."

"Where's Leroy?"

Harold jerked his head in the direction of the Coast Guard cutter. "They got a big flap going out there. They pulled this guy up in the strait, so Leroy says the Coast Guard should have him. The Coast Guard says since they fished him out near South Beach, he belongs to us."

Apparently Leroy lost the argument. Scott found him, head bent in thought beside the draped body. "Harold said you had a problem."

"Talk about Murphy's Law," he said. "Old Doc Miles is out on a case on the west side, Frank's on the mainland—hours before he gets back—and I have to ID this bird, check him against missing persons in Canada." He outlined the tasks that were his, which, by Scott's calculations, would take him the rest of the night and then some. "Oh, hell," he said finally, lifting his big hands in disgust. "Sorry, Doc, didn't mean to unload on you."

Since it was unlike the big man to "unload" on anybody, Scott guessed he was tired to the point of exhaustion, and, considering the events of recent days, understandably. The sheriff and his small staff were being strained to the limit.

"How can I help?" Scott said.

"I know the water changes the rate of deterioration, but could you give me a ballpark guess on when this guy died?"

"Let's have a look."

Leroy drew a deep sigh. "It's not a pretty one." He lifted the tarp.

Scott drew in his breath. It wasn't a pretty one. The carnivorous creatures of the sea had worked him over badly enough to make identification a serious problem. It wasn't that, however, that brought the sharp pull at Scott's chest. The dead man was wearing a torn and seaweed-crusted, but still clearly yellow, slicker, exactly like the one on the man who'd disappeared from the stern of the *Pilgrim*.

He was tall, well built, white male, late thirties. Beyond that, however, all Scott could tell with certainty was that he had chestnut hair. Scott tried to put a time on tissue decay that had been partially slowed by the cold salt water. He tried to spot injury marks. This, too, was difficult with so much tissue missing. The head, or what remained of it, was bloated and like pulp, nothing to tell from it without extensive examination. He unfastened the torn pieces of jacket. No wounds on the upper torso. He probed as much as he thought he should without making the coroner's work more difficult. It all fit, but he couldn't be sure.

"Seen enough?" Leroy said.

Scott nodded, and Leroy quickly threw the cover back.

"How long do you think he's been in the water?" Leroy continued.

"Four days, I should think."

"Between four and six, or two and four?"

It was time to tell Leroy what he'd seen that night. "If my hunch is right, he's been in the water exactly four days."

Leroy looked puzzled. "Run that by me again."

"It might sound a little wild."

"Doc, nothing could sound wild to me tonight."

Scott told him about the *Pilgrim* and the three men on the afterdeck and finished with, "I didn't actually see them throw him over, but it looked like someone had gone in, so I followed the ship out of sight. Never saw the man in the yellow slicker again."

Leroy stared quietly at his shoelaces.

Scott had no idea if Leroy thought the story plausible or off the wall. "Well?" Scott said, beginning to get an uncomfortable feeling it was the latter.

"He could've gone below, couldn't he?"

Off the wall it was. "Until tonight, that's what I thought," Scott said. "But at the time I didn't think so, and after the run-ins with those two—"

Leroy groaned. C'mon, Doc, you're not going to tell me it was the two clowns from the Whaler."

He was, of course, going to say exactly that. "I told you it would sound crazy."

Leroy removed his hat and wiped his brow. "No—didn't mean that. It's just—well, hell, half the people on this island have yellow weather gear, and you say yourself from the distance you couldn't see their faces." Leroy sighed. "Not that seeing *his* face would do any good. So what about the time?"

"I still say three or four days. No way you can be sure without a thorough examination." Yes, Scott thought vengefully, leave it to the coroner. If he says the man died of a skull fracture, then maybe Leroy will be ready to listen. "If you're sending out notices to Canada, I'd list it as three to six. That should cover you pretty well."

Leroy nodded satisfaction. On the cause of death, he was content with accidental drowning.

"There again, you'll have to wait," Scott cautioned. "There's always the possibility of heart arrest, seizure, a blow to the head."

Leroy grinned. "Okay, Doc. Anything else?"

Scott confessed he'd found nothing definite, nothing to confirm his suspicions, and, certainly, injuries were to be expected in a fall, not to mention the bumping around the body received being pulled out by the fishermen. Any bruises or contusions would be hardly conclusive at this point.

"It's probably the wrong time to ask," Scott said, "but how are you coming on your other investigations?"

"Did I tell you we found shotgun shells in the old radar station? Looks like they match up with the ones that killed Owen."

"Odd, to shoot a man and leave the evidence only a few hundred yards away."

Leroy stuck his hands in his pockets and stared absently at the blanketed body on the deck. "Guess they had no reason to hurry."

"Unless they came by boat and left the same way. Maybe someone interrupted them, and they ducked into the radar station and waited until it was safe and then left in their boat." Scott was thinking of the Whaler.

"No evidence of a boat."

"It was a high tide that night."

Leroy smiled knowingly. The Whaler had been stolen after the murder, he pointed out.

"Look," Scott said, "I admit I didn't see them clearly, but there are other ways of identifying people."

"Such as?"

"Body build, physical aberrations."

"Did they have any?"

"The one who ran the boat, the one called Charlie, had a congenital hip problem, walked with a slight limp."

"What about the chase out there in the channel? Did you get a good look at them then?"

"I was busy, but Erin did. She saw them when they came into the restaurant, too. I'll bring her in tomorrow. You can ask her. The two from the Whaler are the same two from the break-in, I'm sure of that."

Scott slept fitfully, and not just because of Leroy's doubts.

78

The gill-netter traffic was particularly heavy, and the noise of the diesels, combined with those brilliant flashes off Iceberg Point, like someone shining a flashlight in his room all night, made sleep difficult.

At first he thought the blinking lights came from the Iceberg beacon, but he soon observed they ran in tandem and were much brighter, sometimes like the blips on a sonar screen, sometimes like lightning bolts that stopped for a while and then struck again when you were sure they wouldn't.

He didn't remember sleep when it came, only remembered the dream, the one where Toni walked down the beach, her long black hair unfettered and flowing free. Only this time clownlike faces without eyes floated around her. He called to her, and she began to run. Suddenly, from behind the rocks two men appeared and pounded down the pebbled tide flats after her. Scott chased them, but as he raced over the sand his feet began to sink into the pools of mud. The harder he ran the deeper he sank, until he couldn't move at all, could only watch helplessly while the two men picked Toni up and tossed her over the rocks like a rejected fish into the rolling sea.

Scott woke wringing wet. He ran his hand over the sheets, confirmed he was in bed, alone, and Toni was gone. Shivering, he snapped on the bedlight and squinted at the clock. Three! Too early to get up, but the prospect of another dream was more than he could face.

It was quiet in the room except for Dandy's heavy breathing and the rippling of water running over the rocks below the deck. The wind had subsided considerably, so only a gentle breeze blew through the screen, and even the lights from Lopez had stopped sending their unwelcome signals through his window. Scott swung his feet over the side of the bed and forced himself up. He padded into the bathroom, turned on the tap, and splashed cold water on his face.

He walked barefoot to the study, scanned the bookshelves, and selected an intriguing title, a book Fred had given him for Christmas, *How to Profit in Stocks and Bonds*. He'd given

serious consideration to stock trading as an alternative to medicine and had accumulated several books on the subject, but so far
hadn't been able to concentrate on any of them.

"This one's a sure winner," Fred promised.

He took the book back to bed with him. Dandy stirred,
looked up, saw Scott in bed, and promptly went back to sleep.
Scott finally found his own antidote for insomnia. He read only a
few moments before he, too, fell asleep, this time without
dreams.

Eleven

Erin and Al had heard about the body at South Beach.

"It's on all the morning news," Al said. "Some darn fool out there in a little boat. See it all the time. They got no respect for these waters, don't have the foggiest idea what they're doing."

Reminded of yesterday's stupidity, Scott abandoned any thought of telling them about the *Pilgrim*, and he and Erin set out for the sheriff's office.

Erin had a sharp memory for detail. She described the driver of the Whaler as a man of about thirty-six, not very tall, round face, tendency to overweight, ruddy complexion, and wispy sand-colored hair.

"Wispy?"

"Not much of it."

A limp? On this point she wasn't certain. She had noticed a tattoo on his right forearm. One of those symbols like the marines wear.

This evoked a lifted eyebrow from Leroy.

She described the second man as in his early twenties, tough, all bone and muscle, mostly bone, "mean eyes," black hair, permed.

Leroy screwed up his face. "Permed?"

"I may be wrong, but it didn't look like natural curl to me."

Leroy wrote it all down, but Scott thought it was more to please Erin, that he had already closed the book on those two. As for Owen, the only real lead so far, he said, was turning up the mask in Victoria. "So I think I'll call this expert of yours, this Brice Randall."

"What about the museum curator?" Scott said.

"She's out of town for a whole month. Not as many experts on that stuff as you might think."

Back on the street, Erin didn't appear to share Scott's feelings that Leroy had little interest in finding the two men. As they strolled down Spring Street she was still trying to recall little things about the two. When they reached the corner, she wondered if Scott was in a hurry. She wanted to check out the yarn shop.

He left her at the shop and headed out on the road to the university's experimental lab on the north shore of the harbor.

The long wooded drive into the five-hundred-acre facility opened up around the central building that housed the tanks. Here the biochemists and fisheries people studied marine plant and invertebrate sea life. Below the main research building were the docks that harbored the university vessels. A float plane was tied up to the inside dock, and beyond it were a couple of runabouts. The rest of the piers were empty. On the hillside overlooking the docks was the staff housing for faculty, visiting scientists, and the students who rotated through the center as part of their classwork.

Scott parked the Jeep and strolled over to the main building. He found Preston in the lab, wearing heavy-rimmed reading glasses as he examined a tank full of sea anemones. In the year since he'd last seen him, Preston hadn't changed. He still could have passed for thirty, though he was Scott's age. He was about six feet, sparely built, with a well-shaped face and thick, carefully groomed dark brown hair. He was good-looking and knew it, intelligent and knew that, too. He came from a wealthy Long Island family and had been eastern school trained. Scott had first met him when he was in graduate school at the university. The women had pursued him in those days, but as far as Scott knew he'd remained a bachelor.

Preston was wearing designer jeans and an expensive soft-collared shirt. He had the kind of face that seldom showed surprise. When he saw Scott he rose from his chair and rationed a half-smile. "Scott, been a while." He still spoke with the accent of the eastern well-off. He reached out slowly to accept Scott's outstretched hand.

Preston had heard about Owen. He leaned against a fish tank and stared off through the big windows at the harbor. He hadn't seen the attorney in months, he said, "but Owen was a man who made enemies without effort." He had no new ideas on the murder. His work kept him out of touch and tied down.

"You here for the summer?"

Preston nodded. "I'm senior resident. Corny is on sabbatical in Australia, so that leaves me." His sigh suggested the responsibility placed an unwanted burden on him. Since Scott knew taking Dean Cornwell's place, even for the summer, was bound to boost Preston's standings, he found the marine biologist's attitude amusing.

"You're next in line for top dog, then?"

Preston acknowledged this was "probably" true, sounding as though the whole prospect bored him immensely.

"Your work must cut into your social life."

Preston showed the first trace of a real smile. "Until recently it's been almost nonexistent, but I'm working on it."

"You missed Owen's last party. I thought you and Owen were such pals."

Scott said it in a teasing voice, but Preston had never had a sense of humor. His smile vanished. "Owen was a crude, disgusting man who took advantage of everyone he ever met. He was no friend of mine."

It was a strong indictment from a man who seldom ventured a strong opinion. Scott also remembered Preston had gone to the parties in the old days, that he, like most of the people on the Cape, used to regard Owen as a generous host and took it as a high honor to be on his guest list. Preston had his guard up now. Scott felt the force of those intense eyes, watching and waiting, waiting for the one question that had stood between them these many months. The question formed on the edge of Scott's tongue about Toni, his mind already dreading the answer. "I—ah—was looking over your docks. Where are all the big ships?" It wasn't the question Scott intended, the one he still couldn't bring himself to ask.

"We're running only the small ones around here this summer."

"What about the *Pilgrim*?"

Preston followed the path of the big *Kaleetan* ferry that was docking in the harbor. "We chartered her for the summer. She's in Campbell River at the moment."

"Kind of unusual to use a schooner in your research, isn't it?"

"It's experimental this year. Our big ships were delayed in Panama, and the people who own the *Pilgrim* came along with an offer we couldn't refuse."

"A popular decision with the students, I imagine."

"We had no trouble getting volunteers," Preston agreed with another faint smile.

"So the students crew?"

Preston turned cagy. "Officially, no."

"Has the ship been in Canada long?"

"Quite some time, yes."

Scott traced a pattern on the glass tank with his finger. "That's funny. I thought I saw her run through here last week."

The dark eyes flickered. "Yes, that's right. They ran down for a few days and left again."

Preston seemed reluctant to discuss the operation of the *Pilgrim* except on the sketchiest of terms, and Scott finally gave up. He didn't want to arouse Preston's curiosity. He asked about the lab and people they both knew and tried to make it appear this had been a social call. He must have succeeded, because Preston began looking at his watch, a clear sign he was losing interest and wanted to return to his work. Scott finally left him with his question still unanswered. Preston returned to the sea anemones and didn't look up as Scott let himself out the door.

Erin made her purchases at the yarn shop, and Scott suggested lunch at Roche Harbor on the other side of the island. Built on the site of an old lime quarry, the resort maintained an historic hotel that once was a Hudson's Bay trading post and a restaurant that overlooked the bay. A white-steepled church sat on the hill, and a short distance away were the tennis courts and the swimming pool. Mostly, it was a haven for boaters. The cruisers and sailors stacked in, side by side, across a long dock in front of the restaurant, and beyond the docks, more boats sat at anchor, their masts and counting towers stretching across half the bay. Scott found a carefree atmosphere here that was less in evidence in Friday Harbor where the townspeople took themselves more seriously.

Roche basked a brilliant blue in the summer sun, not a wind ripple in the entire bay. Scott and Erin sipped clear white Chablis from tall goblets and watched the boats come and go. A group of pleasure cruisers started in around Henry Island, coming past Center Reef on the long way from Speiden Channel. A few smaller boats ran the closer passage around Davison Head on Pearl's east corner, which prompted Erin's observation.

"Why didn't all the boats take the shortcut?"

"There's a treacherous rock outcropping out there that surfaces only at slack tide. I've seen a dozen props twisted out of shape on that little shortcut."

Erin's gaze shifted to the long passage. A tall ship, sixty or seventy feet, had turned around the jetty and was motoring toward customs.

"Beautiful. Looks a little like the *Pilgrim*."

"Except the *Pilgrim*'s a schooner. This one's a yawl."

She nodded. "That slanted topsail reminds me of buccaneers. I remember thinking that when the *Pilgrim* went through Cattle Pass last summer. By the way," she said, "is it much of a sail to Victoria?"

"Not long with a stiff wind." He emphasized the "stiff," and they both broke up laughing. People at nearby tables began to stare.

"Sorry." Erin stifled another giggle. "Wasn't funny yesterday, though, was it?"

She was, he thought, the sort of girl who would always laugh a lot.

"Do you think Leroy will ever find Owen's killer?"

"Hard to say. Leroy does a good job, but in many ways his hands are tied. His jurisdiction is the islands. Sooner or later everything goes off the islands—killers, thieves, and their booty. That makes Leroy far more dependent on the police in other areas than most law-enforcement people."

She looked into her wineglass. "As you say, the sheriff can't very well go off island to chase these people, and the authorities in other areas have their own priorities, probably don't give a hoot about San Juan Island. That's an idea, isn't it? I mean, there's nothing to stop you and me, and it could be fun to poke around ourselves."

"What had you in mind?" he said warily.

She traced a circle on the table mat with her fork. "The antique shop in Victoria."

"Do you know where it is?"

"No, but there can't be too many antique shops in downtown Victoria, and we could ask."

Scott laughed. It wasn't likely Leroy would tell. He was digesting her proposal when she pointed to the finger docks directly below them. "The yawl is tying up."

"Would you like to walk along the docks and get a closer look?"

"Oh, yes, let's do."

They were admiring the tall ship when Scott felt manicured fingernails wrap around his wrist like Archimedes' claws. "Scott!" It was Marilyn Delaney in bright red shorts, smiling at him. "Bob, see who's here!"

From the flying bridge of the shiny white Tollycraft, Bob Delaney appeared, holding the ever-present highball glass. He was wearing a brightly flowered Hawaiian shirt and Bermuda shorts, which didn't quite cover the knobby knees or fully hide a stomach that was beginning to press the limits of its belt. He hadn't changed much since the last time Scott had seen him a year ago. His brown hair under the captain's hat looked a little thinner, but he had the same fleshy face, nicely tanned, with a few more lines. Sunglasses covered his eyes. As always, his smile flashed automatically, the tool of the salesman who took his work wherever he went.

He climbed down from his boat, still holding the highball. Marilyn tugged Scott the remaining few feet, and Bob stuck out his free hand. Scott gripped it. It was wet, cold, and soft to the touch. He smelled strongly of bourbon and after-shave.

"Hi. C'mon aboard. I'll fix you a drink."

"Bob," Marilyn said, "I promised Scott a run in the boat."

"Sure—good idea."

"No—no," Scott protested, reaching behind him for Erin. "We were really just going."

Marilyn's hands moved faster to reclaim his arm than Scott could move away from them. Erin watched in amusement. "Erin," Scott said, "I think you remember Marilyn and Bob Delaney. Al Turner's granddaughter, Erin."

"Nice to see you again," Erin said, still smiling.

"Where you been hiding?" Bob said, taking her hand and steering her toward the boat.

The Delaney cabin was surprisingly roomy for a twenty-six-foot boat, well furnished with stove, refrigerator, sink, table, and cushioned benches. The walls were bare except for a picture of Bob getting a Rotary award for community service. On the bulkhead over the sink was a small Apple computer that, Scott guessed, housed Bob's real estate listings and other sales data. A nice layout. Bob must do pretty well at sales, Scott thought.

Erin said they'd sailed yesterday.

"I hope you didn't get caught in the squall," Marilyn said. "That stuff scared the skinny out of me. Bob looked at the barometer, and it was blowing thirty-five knots, and he said to hell with it, let's stay put. We tied up here and bounced like tops all night. Didn't sleep a wink."

"Wind's no problem for a sailboat," Scott said, and Erin bit back another attack of the giggles.

With the dark glasses removed, Bob's pale-brown eyes were watery and vague as they tried to focus on Scott's face. "Bourbon or vodka?"

"Bourbon with water, thanks."

"Same," Erin said.

Bob performed his bartending chores like a man happy with his work and delivered the drinks to Scott and Erin.

"You didn't fix me one," Marilyn said, none too sweetly.

Dutifully, Bob took her glass, poured in a large portion of vodka, added tomato juice, returned it to her, and sat down, looking like a man with a problem.

"How's the real estate business?" The way he brightened to the question, Scott guessed business wasn't the problem.

"I closed a big condo deal yesterday."

"How's raw land doing?"

"Great. If you're interested, got some real nice buys." In a voice starting to slur, Bob described an assortment of parcels, estimating prices so liberally that Scott imagined they came more out of the Seagram's bottle than the computer that sat over his head.

Bob finished his drink and rolled the ice cubes around the glass, touched one with his tongue, and let it slide back to the bottom. "Another?"

"No, thanks."

"What kin' of property you lookin' for?" Bob said, returning to the sink.

"Acreage."

"Ah—hobby farm. Tax dodge, huh?"

Marilyn, who was adept in the wifely practice of following two conversations at the same time, burst in. "Tell him about Canada. Bob's got some great buys on Vancouver Island, horse ranches, mining properties."

Bob's flaccid face twitched. "Marilyn, butt out."

She didn't take the suggestion well, and Erin glanced uncomfortably across at Scott while husband and wife glared at each other. Marilyn lightened up first. "C'mon," she said to Erin, "let's you and I sit on the deck and let them talk business."

Erin looked relieved as she followed Marilyn out of the cabin.

"Canada, is it?" Scott said to Bob. I've been interested in property on Vancouver Island for years."

Bob was now having great difficulty focusing. "If you like, I can show you pieces 'round Nanaimo that'll knock your eyes out."

"I was thinking more about Campbell River."

Bob's fingers lost their grip on the glass, and ice and bourbon spilled all over the carpet. Scott reached for the paper towel and started mopping up. Bob watched, saying nothing. "There." Scott sponged the last drop. "I think I've got it all."

Bob shook his head as though he were just coming out of a trance. "Campbell River? Why ya' want anything up there? Your resale won't be worth shit."

"I've always liked the wilderness," Scott said truthfully, handing Delaney the empty glass.

Delaney gripped the table for support. "Tell you, Doc, my memory's fuzzy today. How 'bout if I look up the listings and give you a call?"

Erin was quiet on the drive home. It was the Delaneys, Scott thought darkly, spoiling a perfect afternoon. Scott turned onto Valley Road, where the foliage opened up from the densely forested parkland onto fields, farmhouses, and mud ponds. "The Delaneys are a trial," he said apologetically, "particularly when they're drinking."

"Marilyn's very friendly. Bob travels a lot. I imagine she drinks because she gets lonesome. Did you know Marilyn has been very worried about you?"

She might have said, "Did you know your house is on fire?" Scott looked at her in surprise, and the Jeep lurched toward the center stripe. He drew back into their lane. "Where did she come up with that?"

"I assumed she was talking about . . . about your wife's death," Erin said in a small voice.

He resented being the subject of Marilyn's gossipy tongue. "Her husband's got it right," he said in a terse voice. "Marilyn talks too much." He gripped the wheel tighter and took the curve a little faster than he'd intended.

"Is it hard to talk about her? About your wife, I mean?"

"Why should it be?"

She sighed. "I'm sorry. I shouldn't have brought it up."

"No reason to be sorry. What else did good old Marilyn have to say?"

"Not much."

"Don't stop now. It sounds like you two had a jolly good gabfest at my expense." Once the words were out, childish, angry, there was no way to reclaim them.

"If you really want to know," she said with an anger to match his own, "Marilyn thought Toni was beautiful and spoiled and the kind who didn't care about anyone's feelings except her own. Satisfied?"

The words stung, but he'd heard them before. Ralph had said it often enough, and Lorene, and they'd lost their capacity to shock. Erin's anger started to soften his own. "Satisfied," he said meekly.

She was quiet until they turned onto the Cape road. As they rounded the bend by American Camp and started through the grove of pine trees, she finally spoke. "You're right," she said, looking down at her hands, "it wasn't any of my business."

Twelve

Fred and Lorene were back on the island and turning everything upside down as usual. Scott felt his answering voice go flat on the phone. "Hi, Fred. Good to have you back."

If Fred noticed Scott's lack of enthusiasm, he gave no sign of it. Business was fine, he boasted. He'd taken a spread in wheat that had paid off handsomely, but he quickly added that making money wasn't everything. Scott stopped a laugh.

"We want you to be a fourth for bridge tonight," he said when he finally got the preliminaries out of the way.

"You know I hate bridge, Fred."

"C'mon, Scottie, Lorene asked Cynthia. She's counting on you to fill out the table. You can't let her down."

"I'm not interested in getting anything on with Cynthia, Fred." If the truth were known, Scott thought, Cynthia probably felt the same way.

"Come over for a cup of coffee, and let's talk."

"Fred, you haven't heard a word I've said."

On the outside, Fred and Lorene's house was like the other ramblers on the Cape—cedar siding stained in sand tones, large windows. Inside, it was expensively furnished, generally in good taste, but always cluttered. Lorene, who'd had everything done for her as a child of wealthy parents, had never learned to keep house. Thanks to Millie, who came in once a week, there was no dust and the floors were clean, but the tables and chairs were always piled high with magazines, Fred's business papers, and pamphlets from Lorene's community projects. Their golf clubs nearly always stood in a corner of the entry hall, probably deposited there weeks earlier, since Fred and Lorene were only sporadic golfers. Generally, the place always looked in need of a good shoveling out.

Fred didn't seem to mind Lorene's lapses in the housekeeping department, for had he cared enough to say anything, Lorene would have moved heaven and earth to change her ways. Pleasing Fred had always been her life's passion. "She smothers poor Fred," Toni had said. If that were the case, Fred was a man who liked being smothered.

In spite of the clutter, it was a warm house, lots of light pouring in from the big windows, particularly in the kitchen, which was most often where they gathered whenever Scott stopped. They sat around the big round table and drank from mugs, and there was nothing here that would have given away that Lorene had grown up a spoiled little rich girl, or that Fred, who'd grown up poor, was now making money hand over fist.

It was Lorene's tendency to get involved with other people's problems that Scott was having trouble with. Lorene had all kinds of other projects, from Campfire Girls and Blood Bank to the Home for Unwed Mothers and the University Drug Abuse Counseling Center. She'd not had children—Fred's decision, according to Cynthia—and had never worked for a salary, not wanted to, according to Lorene herself. So projects it was, and right now, matching Scott with Cynthia Woods was high among these.

Fred waved Scott in with a grin. Lorene was in the kitchen at work over the sink. She was dressed in her usual tight blue jeans, which did little to hide the extra pounds she always complained about, and a pale blue smock. The sink overflowed with pots and bowls. She looked distracted, a normal condition, and happy to see Scott, which instantly made him feel guilty. He stepped over a box of unpacked clothes and weaved a path to her side.

"Scottie!" Her wet fingers dug into his shoulders as she

hugged him. Her green eyes shone brighter than usual. She planted a kiss on his cheek.

"You're looking good," Scott said, easing himself from her arms.

Fred dropped into a chair at the table. "Lorene, fix us some coffee."

Scott looked for a chair that wasn't piled high with papers, and not seeing one, moved a stack of magazines to the floor and sat next to Fred. Dandy found his favorite corner by the refrigerator, which quickly proved a judicious choice, because Lorene had saved him a piece of steak from their dinner. Dandy accepted the gratuity with a friendly wag of his tail, and Lorene placed a kettle of water on the burner.

She was on a new kick about her coffee, grinding it herself and using a different method of brewing. She busied herself with this while Fred insisted on hearing every grisly detail of Owen's murder. Lorene paused now and again to moan or gasp as Scott described the murder scene. The fact that it had occurred only a few feet from their front door clearly had jolted them both.

It was on Scott's lips to tell Fred about his own break-in, but remembering his promise to Leroy and not anxious to upset them further, he told Fred only Al's theories about the murder and about the missing death mask. "Al doesn't think one mask is motive for murder."

"Why? I thought those clown faces were worth a fortune."

"They are, or at least I think they are. Here I see Al's point. Why leave most of them there?"

"Maybe the killer was scared off." Fred leaned back in his chair and rested his short legs on a stack of newspapers. "Hey, Scottie, 'member when a bunch of the guys lifted the bones out of old Worthington's anthro lab and strung them up in the living room of the Kappa house?"

Lorene's laugh sounded like a shriek as she recalled the incident.

"As my memory serves me, they blamed it on the med students."

Fred laughed. "Too bad you missed all the fun, ol' buddy."

Scott smiled at the memory of Fred constantly in the middle of every fraternity prank, and a feeling of affection for his friend swept over him.

Lorene took some sweet rolls out of the freezer and set them in the oven, nodding occasional interest in the conversation. Fred went back to dissecting Owen's murder, with questions about the position of the body and the nature of the wound. Scott couldn't remember his friend ever taking so much interest in anatomy.

On the stove the coffeepot threatened to boil over. Lorene removed it from the burner and began pushing down frantically on a knob at the top of the glass. A strong aroma of fresh-brewed coffee floated across the room.

"I can't wait for you to try this, Scottie," she said. "It's Swiss, or maybe it's French. Anyway, you plunge the coffee through the water and then you put a glob of cream on top, and it comes out positively yummy." She rolled her eyes. "I discovered it when I was in Geneva."

Scott glanced at Fred to see if he still smarted at mention of Lorene's solo trip to Europe, a decision of Lorene's that at the time had caused a family crisis. But Fred was screwing up his nose over the coffee.

Lorene's parents had died shortly before that; first her mother, of cancer, and then her father, of a coronary. So Lorene had been anxious to get away. According to Fred, she was tired of vacations on the island and wanted to travel abroad. Fred didn't feel he could leave his business, and Lorene surprised everyone by going anyway. Scott had always thought there was more to it than that, but for whatever reasons, Lorene had gone and from all accounts enjoyed six grand weeks on the Continent.

She'd been different when she returned, a little distant at first. But after Toni died, she and Fred were both so concerned for Scott that she was soon like her old self again. Scott often wondered if, in a grim way, Toni's death had strengthened the bond between Fred and Lorene. Anyway, their crisis had ended.

Right now there was a crisis over the coffee.

Fred moaned. "Not that stuff again."

"Fred, be quiet. Let Scott judge for himself." She took three mugs from a stand on the sink and poured.

With some apprehension, Scott sipped. It was the bitterest stuff he'd ever drunk. "Very nice," he lied, swallowing hard.

Fred looked at him and started laughing. "Liar. My God, Lorene, this tastes worse than the last pot."

Unfazed, Lorene said, "Try the cream, Scottie. I like it, Fred, so get used to it."

Scott laughed at Fred's unhappy face.

"All very fine for you," Fred grumbled, "but I'm stuck with it, and me with an ulcer."

"When did you develop an ulcer?"

"Don't pay any attention to him," Lorene said. "He's just playing on your sympathy. He doesn't have an ulcer."

"I have a nervous stomach," Fred insisted.

Scott smiled. "You're smoking too much."

"Traitor!" Fred stared glumly at his cup.

Lorene went back to the rolls, and Fred poured an extra-large portion of cream into his cup and started talking about Owen again. "That's all that was missing? An African face mask?"

Scott followed Fred's example with the cream. Definitely an improvement. "Unless you count Owen's necklace."

Fred stoppped stirring his coffee. "What necklace was that?"

"You remember, the thing with the spikes? You said it reminded you of a voodoo chain you'd seen when you and Lorene cruised the Caribbean."

Fred nodded. "Yeah, I remember."

"The point is, he wore it all the time, but it wasn't on him when we found him. And according to Erin, it's very valuable."

Lorene looked up from her work at the sink. "Erin?"

"Al Turner's granddaughter, you know the blond kid who used to run around the Cape barefoot?"

Lorene had been beating sugar and water in a small bowl.

She stopped, and with lifted eyebrows said, "She's not a kid, Scottie."

Scott raised his shoulders uncomfortably. "Yes, well, anyway, she's a decorator and knows a little bit about African art. She claims this necklace could be worth a lot, like twenty grand or more."

Fred perked up. "Owen was full of surprises. What happened to it?"

"I suppose the killer snatched it."

Fred sipped thoughtfully from his mug. "So they did take more."

Lorene had no interest in the stolen necklace. "You been seeing much of this girl, Scott?"

Outside, a flurry of seagulls was fighting and screaming over a run of candlefish. "No . . . not much."

"Lorene," Fred said, "mind your own business."

Scott smiled gratefully at his friend. "Say, Fred, what do you know about land in Canada? I ran into the Delaneys, and Bob, well, actually, Marilyn said there were some pretty hot buys up in the Campbell River area. You've a business head; what do you know about that?"

Fred's even face opened up in a grin. "I'm a commodity trader."

"What's the difference, trading in land or commodities?"

Fred sighed tolerantly. "A heap big difference, ol' buddy. Hey, there are a few tricks in my business. You medical men don't have a corner on tough."

Fred was joking, but there was enough behind it to make Scott realize his friend was still sensitive about not finishing college. Scott had been tactless. "Start educating me," he said, smiling sheepishly.

"Scott," Lorene said with the hysterical pitch to her voice she'd acquired recently, "you wouldn't really buy anything on the advice of the Delaneys!"

"Lorene's got a point there."

"No!" Scott shook his head emphatically for Lorene's benefit. "Absolutely no!"

Scott avoided the subject of Cynthia, but Lorene didn't forget. Scott finally took the hardheaded approach. "I'm sorry, Lorene, but I have other plans for this evening."

"All right," Lorene said with a heavy sigh, "but you must come with us to Henry Mason's party next Saturday. Promise?"

"What party?" Scott said.

"You haven't opened your mail," Lorene accused.

He confessed he hadn't looked at it for a day or two. Never anything in it except bills and solicitations, anyway.

"Everyone on the Cape is invited," Lorene said in an excited voice. Henry's celebrating the completion of Santana."

"Santana?"

"That's what he's called his new house. Wonderful, isn't it? He named it after the warm winds that sweep across Southern California from Mexico. His last wife was Spanish, you know. 'Course, the winds on the Cape are hardly what you'd call warm, but the idea's nice. You *must* go, Scottie. Not to would be, well, rude."

Fred looked at Scott and lifted his shoulders in amused silence.

Only when Scott started back in the Jeep did it occur to him this would be the first time everyone on the Cape would be together since Owen's murder, and among Henry's guests would be several who'd been there that fateful night. Then he wondered if Erin would be going, too.

Thirteen

Fish Creek was quiet at early morning. The fishermen were beached again, and the boats swung empty at their slips. Dandy raced ahead of Scott down the pier to the *Nellie J*, barked, and drew no response.

The decks were wet with the morning dew and slick underfoot. Scott stepped lightly. Squealing protests, a gull flew off the piling and found another spot at the opposite end of the docks. Scott leaned on the *Nellie J's* rail and shouted, "Anybody aboard?"

Shortly, Vic, droopy-eyed, stuck his head out of the cabin. The strong smells of beer and whiskey came with him, mixing poorly with the nets, which reeked of dead fish. Vic was hitting the bottle heavier these days.

He grinned when he saw Scott. "Thought it was one of those goddamned Caper's come to bitch about last night."

Scott laughed. "No, just me."

Scott climbed over the rail behind Dandy, who was dancing around the doghouse in search of Georgie. But Georgie, according to Vic, was in town with the rest of the crew, "screwin' off." Vic's mood was improved some over their last meeting, however, and Scott guessed the reason.

"Good catch?"

"Not bad."

"Getting any more time out?"

"Two, three days next week maybe."

They sat on the wet deck, backs against the fish locker, breathing in the fumes of fish, and Vic listened thoughtfully while Scott described what he thought he'd seen that night on the *Pilgrim*, tying it to the incidents with the two men. When Scott finished, Vic grunted, "How about a beer?" He ducked into the cabin and returned with two cans.

"I know it all sounds crazy," Scott said, fearing Vic would agree, "but it was just so real at the time."

Vic uncapped his beer, and foam sprayed his bare arms and spouted in a stream that puddled up on the deck. Dandy licked it dry. "Not crazy at all. Happens more than you might care to think." Vic drank from the can, and froth dribbled down his chin. He wiped it with the back of his hand and released a satisfied sigh. "Reminds me when I was skiffman on a seiner in Alaska. We had a hand who was always mouthing off. Everyone hated his guts. One night we hit seventy-knot winds, lashed everything down, rolled all night and the next. When the wind blew itself out we couldn't find the bastard anywhere. We searched the ship, patrolled the waters. Not a trace." Vic's eyes darkened. "Sure as I'm sitting here, someone pitched him over the side. Couldn't prove it, but everybody knew. It's the same thing in battle. The guy that gives everyone a hard time draws first fire. Who checks to see if the bullets hit his back or his chest? Had a shavetail lieutenant went out that way."

"You think this could be the same sort of deal?"

Vic scratched his head. "One thing different. Up north you're far from everything. Hard to check up. In Korea everyone was getting shot up, so who was keeping count? But to pitch someone overboard right in the middle of Cattle Pass strikes me as pretty dumb. You'd think they'd at least wait until they're in open waters. If you're thinking of trying to convince Leroy, I'd say forget it."

Vic didn't mean it as a rejection, but Scott was disappointed nonetheless.

Vic finished off the beer and went below, returning with

another. Scott drank from his first. It was warm, and settled poorly on his empty stomach. He set it down beside him on the deck. "Do you happen to know who owns the *Pilgrim*, Vic?"

"A Canadian outfit, I think."

"I suppose it's a matter of record with the Canadian Coast Guard."

Vic laughed. "When you want to know something like that, you don't ask the fuckin' Coast Guard. You ask another fisherman. I'll check around."

"While you're doing that, maybe you can find out who's been blinking their floods off Iceberg the past few nights. Damn things are keeping me awake."

Instantly serious, Vic came up with his standard answer to all unexplained trouble. "Fuckin' Indians."

"Don't think so. First I thought it was the lighthouse lamp, but it blinks out of sync, goes on for several minutes, on and off, and then quits."

"Sounds like the navy signal ships."

This struck a thought buried somewhere.

Boots shuffled on the ramp, and Vic raised his head. "Hey, here's the man who'd know. Why don't you ask Billy?"

Billy Leroux, black hair, tall, rod-slender, stepped lightly down the steeply sloped ramp and flashed the familiar white smile. "Hi, Vic, Doc." Then, looking at the green-quilted rocks on the beach, "Tide's out. Should be good fishing."

"Billy, you're full of shit," Vic said.

Billy's laugh was high-pitched and happy. Billy was a local half-breed who ran a gill-netter, the *Billy Jean*, which, since the court ruling, was officially considered an Indian boat. He and Vic had been friends long before the treaty, but this didn't stop Vic from being bitter when Billy went out and Vic had to sit ashore. Billy rested his lean brown arms on Vic's rail and, still grinning, said, "Ask Billy what?"

"Why are those Indian boats signaling each other all night long? They're keeping the Doc here awake."

Billy blinked bewilderment, and Scott explained about the lights.

Billy looked at Vic, his black eyes amused. "You think the Indians are sending smoke signals with their floods? Don't be dumb, Vic. Hey, even the Indians have radios." Billy had no explanation for the flashing lights, but he had seen the *Pilgrim* the day of the fog. "She nearly ran me down. We were heading outta Shaw."

"How do you know it was the *Pilgrim*?" Vic said sourly.

"Hey, I know that boat. My boys went out on her with the Sea Scouts. Don't know the turkey who's running her this year, but he's not long on brains. It was so foggy in the strait you couldn't see your feet, and this guy barrels through there like he's running the Indianapolis Five Hundred."

"Did you see where they went?"

"Not sure, but I'd have punched him out if I'd caught up with him." Two of Billy's crew started down the ramp carrying Thermos bottles and duffel bags. They nodded silent greetings to Vic and Scott and climbed aboard Billy's boat. "That's my signal to go," Billy said.

While Vic watched glumly, Billy backed up his gill-netter and, waving, took off out of the creek, stirring a giant white trail behind him. Scott laid a hand on his friend's shoulder. "I know what you're thinking, Vic, but remember, it's not Billy's fault."

"Not mine either," Vic said unhappily.

By late afternoon the fog moved into Cattle Pass with the same swiftness as on the night of the *Pilgrim* encounter, covering the rocks and the water like a milky blanket, heavy, cool, and damp. The gray outside world quickly permeated Scott's rooms. Scott looked at the dishes piled up in the sink and decided dinner could wait. He opened a box of crackers, fed some to the dog, munched one himself. He poured a glass of sherry, put on a Mozart wind concerto, and settled down in the big leather chair with the book on stock-trading techniques. Dandy curled up on the floor at his feet, and Scott read. In less than twenty minutes, he was asleep.

Dandy's barking played faintly on his subconscious before he jumped awake, aware someone was ringing the bell. He opened the door, and there was Erin, smiling back at him. Blinking away sleep, he tucked his shirt in, brushed his hair with his hand, and felt as awkward as he had on his first date.

"I wonder if I could borrow a cup of sugar," she said.

Fully awake, he threw the door open wide and waved her in. "A whole pound, if you like."

She burst out laughing. "It's not true, about the sugar. I saw you were alone, and Grandpa and I hoped you'd join us for dinner. Grandpa's tired of just me underfoot, and wishes you'd come."

She selected her borrowings—a bottle of sauterne and a cube of butter—and he and Dandy followed her out the door like spaniels after a duck.

Dinner was veal tenderloin, new potatoes, and greens, and Scott was certain no meal had ever tasted better. He and Al ate shamefully huge portions while Erin talked and picked at her food. She was excited; he could see that from the sparkle in her eyes. She had news, she said, about the African death masks. "I talked to Brice Randall on the phone this afternoon, and guess what?"

Scott shook his head unenthusiastically.

"It's the most amazing coincidence. He saw Owen's collection only three weeks ago at one of Owen's parties. Fact is, he wanted to buy some of the pieces, but Owen wouldn't sell. He said they're definitely of high quality."

"So is he coming to take another look?"

"He can't get away just now, but I talked to the sheriff, and he says if Brice says they're authentic, that's good enough for him. He says they can appraise them anytime."

Scott was surprised at Leroy.

It was quickly clear Erin had something else on her mind. Far from forgetting about going to Victoria to look for the antique shop where Owen's killer had unloaded the stolen face mask, she was now more firmly fixed on the idea.

"How about it, Al?" Scott said, winking knowingly at the old man. "Give Erin a chance to do a little shopping."

"That's not the idea at all," Erin said huffily, starting to clear the table.

Scott spent the next ten minutes apologizing, while Al smiled and stoked up his pipe.

Fourteen

They left Al slumped contentedly over his typewriter. In happy spirits, they caught the midmorning ferry to Sidney and drove the twenty-minute distance into downtown Victoria.

The *Princess Marguerite* from Seattle was just docking in the Inner Harbor to deliver its daily mass of visitors as Scott parked the Jeep. Luxury yachts and sailboats of the clipper class stood at rest in the sun. Everything else around the stone breakwater was in motion—tourists walking briskly down Government Street, the London double-decker buses rumbling back and forth, and the Tally-ho horse carriages clopping past the Empress Hotel, whose steeply pitched slate roofs and ivy-covered brick and stone columnades among green lawns and hanging flower baskets had stood over the harbor since the turn of the century.

In the bustling lobby of the Empress, they plotted their next move.

"All we know for certain," Erin said, "is that the mask turned up in an antique shop in downtown Victoria. We have no name and no address. That could make it tough."

Scott grinned. "I have complete confidence in you."

"Go ahead and laugh, but I do have a plan."

The plan amounted to walking through downtown Victoria, stopping in all the antique shops until they came upon the right one. According to Erin, very few antique shops dealt in African artifacts. She'd been surprised, she said, at the mask turning up at one in the first place. "Most of the good stuff comes out of auctions, and most of those are held in New York, London, or Paris."

They started their hunt on Government Street, intent on working their way north and west, and back to the hotel. Erin walked evenly at Scott's side, her eyes on every shop, passing up woolens and yarns with regretful glances. When she spotted a little shop in Trounce Alley with a display of women's accessories, he insisted they go in.

Erin admired a counter layered with a cheerful assortment of silk scarves. "Pick one," he said.

"I shouldn't."

He selected one on the top with geometric patterns in blazing reds and brilliant blues and held it against her face. "Matches your eyes."

"Didn't you know I'm a summer?"

Scott went blank. "Something out of the decorator's lexicon, right?"

She laughed. "Everyone has a group of colors that best suits their coloring." She studied his face. "Fair hair, blue eyes. You're a spring," she decided. "Your best colors are beige, browns, blues."

"So what colors are yours?"

"Pinks, pastels."

"Mmm. So, we'll find one more to your suiting." He reached for another of the silk squares.

She stopped him. "Don't you dare. I want this one." She held the silk to her face and rubbed it against her skin and laughed. "I've always loved bright colors."

"If I live to be a hundred," he said, shaking his head at her logic. He made the purchase, and they left the shop in high spirits. "To business," he said. She took his arm, and in this determined manner, they proceeded onto the side streets of downtown Victoria.

She found her first prospect in a cloistered little place off

Pandora Street that specialized in Eskimo sculpture. Scott pointed to a window full of stone and whalebone carvings and expressed the view that it appeared slightly afield of African art.

"Yes," Erin said, "but the point is they deal in artifacts, not just old china and chairs. Trust me."

He bowed to her superior knowledge, and they went in. The proprietor was a gaunt-looking woman in her mid-thirties. She had coal-black hair, pale skin, and dark, distant eyes. Erin started to explain her interest in African artifacts. The woman didn't wait for her to finish.

"You can find Indian artifacts here in Victoria, but I can't imagine where you would find any of African derivation. We deal exclusively in the works of the Eskimos." There was a definite condescension in her manner.

Erin left with her defensive shoulders up. "That woman acted like we were total amateurs."

"In my case, it's quite true," Scott said.

They walked through alleys and small shopping malls, and finally they found one in another out-of-the-way corner, which Erin pronounced "authentic."

To Scott it looked more like a small art gallery with dusty old prints and a few cracked pots, but Erin said it was typical of the antique business, and she entered with high hopes. The shopkeeper was an older man—gray hair, gray face, gray eyes, three-piece gray suit, and a manner like the winter fog on the Cape. Scott was more than content to leave him wholly to Erin.

"I'm an interior decorator," Erin began.

Scott traced a finger over a dusty old globe, spun it lightly into orbit. The proprietor shot him a dark look, and Scott stopped the globe's spin and stuck his hands in his pockets.

"I'm on the lookout for a particular piece of African art," Erin continued.

"We deal in English articles."

"This is a face mask."

The gray head moved back and forth. "No, definitely not."

Scott began to wonder how antique dealers made a living.

They started up Yates, continued shop by shop, each dustier than the last, with much the same result. Erin looked at her tourist folder. "I think Fort Street looks like our last best hope."

Fort Street had several galleries and antique dealers. They went to three whose shops were situated very nearly next door to each other, and not one of them knew the first thing about African art. They walked a long block to reach the fourth shop on Erin's dwindling list. It was a little shop that had dirt-clouded windows and smelled suspiciously of rotting wood. A woman of middle age gave them their first real prospect.

"African art? Yes, I believe there was someone around here a few days ago. As I told him, I don't know much about it myself, but I know a dealer who just might."

It was two blocks away, and next door to a yarn shop. "The Stewart McDonald Gallery, Antiques, Gifts, and Tea Rooms. If this isn't it"—Erin held crossed fingers in the air—"I don't know."

Scott gave her an encouraging hug, and, in a mood of resignation, they walked into the tidy little shop. Agnes McDonald, widow of Stewart, was a nice old lady with pale, soft-tissued cheeks, alert brown eyes, and neatly curled gray hair. Erin explained the reason for their visit.

"An African death mask, did you say?"

"A funeral ceremonial, I suppose, would be more accurate. Eighteenth century, I think. As my friend described it, it was a long grotesque face, charcoal, deeply oiled with white across the eyes."

The old lady nodded her head, and Erin squeezed Scott's arm in excitement.

"But I had it only a day, you see. It's gone now."

Erin put on a creditable show of disappointment.

"I'm so sorry," Mrs. McDonald said sympathetically. "You knew, of course, it was only a copy?"

"A copy!" Scott blurted the words in unison with Erin. The surprise this time was genuine.

Erin quickly explained she had her heart set on an original, and Mrs. McDonald accepted this with a shake of her unsuspicious head.

"It was an RCMP matter," the old lady said, and she told them about the solidly built man with the tattooed arm and salty manner who'd brought it in. "He wasn't the sort one associates with collectors. He knew nothing about African artifacts, which naturally aroused my curiosity. In our work we hear about people selling stolen goods. I have to say that for a criminal, he was a gentleman. He swore when I told him what it was worth, but he apologized and didn't put up an argument. Unusual, I think. If you're hoping to get fifty thousand dollars and must settle for a hundred, I imagine some men might become violent over less."

"What happened to the mask?"

"The RCMP impounded it. It's in the States by now." Her milk-white cheeks crinkled in a smile. "It was peculiar from the start. Victoria isn't the place for trading African artifacts. I only deal in an occasional piece because my late husband and I spent some time in Africa. The dealers here are afraid of it."

Erin nodded understanding. "Too much money involved and too easy to be cheated. Only an experienced eye would know if it's from the Gold Coast or the bush, or if it's middle Bennin period or nineteenth century, or if it's been restored or is in its natural state."

The old lady smiled at Erin appreciatively. "Quite so. You have such an interest, I wonder if you would like to see something my husband found on our last trip. It's not for sale, mind, but quite unusual." She slipped into the back of the shop and returned with her prize, a small statuette of a native African bearing a sword. It was a highly polished piece, and at first glance looked to be carved of stone. It turned out to be ebony, crude in its detail but with simple lines, definite style, and, in a curious sort of way, beautiful.

"This is an ancestral statue," she explained. "To the man who carved it, this figurine holds his ancestral spirit." She repeated its history, and Scott began to see African artifacts in a new light. These weren't the ostentatious trappings of an Owen Wentworth, grotesque and gaudy. They were highly individualistic cultural links with the tribes of West Africa and the Congo, with a people and a history about which the Western world still had much to learn. Scott thought of Al's stories of mysterious ruins and ties to the ancients and wished he'd tried harder to persuade him to come today. Then he thought about Owen and his collection. It didn't fit.

"It's beautiful," Erin said with meaning. "If ever you decide to sell it, I'm certain I have a buyer."

They sailed back on the ferry through quiet, moonlit seas. "Think of all the progress we've made," Erin said, pleased with their day's work. "We discovered the mask is a fake."

"Which Leroy undoubtedly already knows and is why he was so anxious to consult an expert."

"Why do you suppose he didn't tell us?"

"Did we confide this trip to him?"

"I see your point. Anyway, now we know something is wrong. I saw those masks of Owen's not more than four months ago, and Brice saw them just a few weeks ago."

"So?"

"Either this mask isn't from Owen's collection or someone switched one of the masks."

"Just one?"

She nodded thoughtfully. "They might have switched more than the one, mightn't they?"

"And what about the man who came into Mrs. McDonald's shop?"

"Charlie, from the Whaler, although I wouldn't have described him as a gentleman. Of course, Mrs. McDonald is such an old dear, she'd not say an unkind word about anyone."

It was after midnight when they arrived back at the Cape. In the soft light of the doorway, her face was still flushed with excitement. "Thank you for the scarf, the wonderful day," she said, giving him a sisterly hug. Her hair brushed his lips, and he got the heady scent of her perfume. "Good night," she whispered and went in. He left with thoughts that were far from fraternal.

Dandy led Scott back to the house in the dark. From his living-room window Scott tracked the waters rising below the deck. Off across the pass, beyond Deadman's Island, the lights still flashed. Dark recesses in the rocks brightened with every flash. He fell hypnotically into its pattern, a long streak followed by a short one, on and off.

Fifteen

Scott woke with Leroy's warnings echoing on his brain. The mask turning out to be a fake underscored the danger, for it pointed to a frustrated killer.

Scott let Dandy out for his early-morning run and stepped barefoot onto the deck behind him. Below the deck where the sun bounced off the water, a seal swam nearly undetected through the thick, brown seaweed, turned, and stared back at Scott through hollow eyes. Until yesterday and Mrs. McDonald's shop, it had all begun to make sense. Now, like a fogged-up window, Scott got a glimmer, but not enough to make a clear pattern. Was it that or was it like putting off telling a patient grim pathological findings? Maybe he didn't want to see where this trail led?

The seal ducked under a patch of kelp in search of the morning offerings of the sea shelf. Dandy sprang back onto the deck, shook the water off his fur, and led the way to the kitchen. "Hungry, boy? Me, too." Scott opened the refrigerator and his hopes died; the dreaded task of grocery shopping could no longer be put off. "We'll stop by Al's and see if he needs anything, and then off we go."

Al shook his head. "Thanks, don't need a thing."

Erin strolled out of the kitchen, greeted Scott with a smile, and talked about their "wonderful day." She then began to write down the items they needed from the store. Scott grinned at the old man, and Al grunted something about "know-it-alls" and reached for his pipe.

"Did Erin tell you about the African mask?"

"Always knew Owen was a phony," Al said. "By the way, I ran into Millie in town yesterday."

Scott said the first thing that came to his head. "Did she know anything about the necklace?"

"I asked her that. Might as well have asked about snow on the moon. She was so upset about her daughter, Prissie, she couldn't talk about anything else."

"What about Prissie?"

"She's missing again."

Erin stopped writing. "You didn't tell me that."

Al shrugged his spiny shoulders. "She ran off. Not the first time. The girl's a perpetual runaway. Didn't want to tell Millie, but it's plain as the nose on my face her daughter has taken up with those potheads on Cady Mountain. Probably up there right now, living in tents and blowing pot."

Erin said, "Isn't anyone doing anything about it?"

"Sure. Leroy's looking, for all the good it'll do. He'll round them up, get her to a counselor. Never accomplishes anything."

Scott had heard about the drug parties on the mountain, which no one on the island seemed able to stop, partly because of the mobility of the kids involved and partly because of a general tendency of the islanders to look the other way. No one wanted to think their kids would get into drugs. In truth, a good number of the drug users were off-islanders.

Al lit his pipe. "I been trying to tell you both, this island is no different than anywhere else. It's all sick."

Erin suggested they get a group of people together and hunt for Prissie. "You can't just write her off. You have to try."

Scott knew the old man felt as badly about the girl as anyone, but his natural pessimism prevented him from raising false hopes. "C'mon, Erin," he said less gruffly, "you can't take on the world's problems. Let the sheriff do his job."

Scott left for town thinking he would add Leroy's office to his stops. There had to be something they could do about poor Prissie.

Friday Harbor was such a small town that Scott never walked down the main street without running into someone he knew. In town, as on the island, people fell into two categories, the full-timers and the summer people, and Scott now felt so much a part of the island's permanent part that he could spot the off-islanders every time.

When he saw the slightly built man in pinstripes coming out of the sheriff's office, he was instantly curious. There was something familiar—and yet different. The line mustache, the dark, almost black hair flecked with silver at the temples, the lean face that had impatience indelibly etched in it. That face didn't belong on the island. It belonged in Seattle, in the boardrooms of the high rises, at the champagne parties.

Scott caught up to him in front of the hardware store. It was Brice Randall all right, and up close, Scott realized what had been different. This wasn't the immaculately groomed, self-assured giant of industry facing him with watery eyes, hair unbrushed, wearing a Bond Street suit that looked like it had gone through a night in the back seat of a car. "Brice Randall, I'll be damned," Scott said.

Brice stared back uneasily. "Scott. What a surprise."

Clearly it was. Besides his nervous manner, his hand lacked a firmness of grip, Scott remembered, and it wasn't hard to see that Brice wasn't at all happy running into Scott. "Been a long time."

"Uh—yes, has, hasn't it? Uh—see you're vacationing. Good idea. Take a little breather from the practice." He glanced at his watch and started to back away, in a hurry to get somewhere.

"What brings you to San Juan Island?"

"Oh . . . sheriff wanted my opinion about Owen Wentworth's art collection."

"What did you think of it?"

Brice shifted uneasily. "Nice. Too valuable to keep in a

summerhouse unprotected. No wonder one of them got lifted."
Brice took another step in the direction of the harbor.

"Then Leroy didn't tell you?"

Brice stopped in his tracks. "Tell me what?"

"That the stolen mask was a copy?"

His mouth dropped open. "They recovered it. No . . . I
guess he forgot to tell me that."

"Did you talk to Erin?"

Brice drew in his breath. "Damn! Knew there was something. You'll be seeing her, won't you? Could you tell her I'll call
first chance I get?"

"Why don't you call her right now? She's home."

He took two more steps to the curb. "Can't . . . plane
waiting. Nice talking to you, Scott . . . sorry I have to run. Let's
get together for coffee sometime . . . been too long." He forgot
to wave as he walked briskly toward the marina and the waiting
plane.

The whole meeting took less than five minutes and left Scott
with questions that had been on the tip of his tongue unanswered, questions about Toni and Owen and that last party at
the store, the last one for Toni ever. Maybe that's why Brice had
been in such a rush.

Scott had never known Brice well. He was Toni's associate,
not Scott's. At the store parties Scott had avoided him whenever
possible, didn't like the way he used a handshake and a smile to
get what he wanted. From the stories Scott had heard, he could
be ruthless when it served his needs. Not a crude manipulator,
like Owen, but with the same lack of concern for whose toes he
crushed.

"He makes it go," Toni argued, obviously admiring the man.

"Smooth," she'd said. Not today. Scott smiled. Wonderful
how the island dropped a man down to size.

Leroy was clearly displeased Scott had run into Brice, and
Scott guessed it was because now Leroy had to explain more than
he'd intended. Leroy tipped back in his swivel chair and looked
up at Scott. "They're all authentic."

"I thought Randall had already vouched for that."

Leroy grinned sheepishly and told him about discovering the mask in Victoria was a fake. Scott decided not to mention that he already knew.

About Prissie, predictably, Leroy had done it all: searched Cady Mountain, the usual hangouts, posted notices in town, interrogated the usual crowd. "They don't talk, these kids. Have a peculiar code of their own. Last time she ran off she moved in with a bunch out near English Camp. Don't worry. We'll find her." On the matter of the man dragged up off South Beach, Leroy still knew nothing. Scott left him poring over a stack of reports, a troubled man fighting a giant wave.

Scott purchased his groceries, stopped by the hardware store and picked up a few more dishes to replace the broken ones, rejoined Dandy in the Jeep, and headed back to the Cape. A breeze started up off the strait and cooled the air. Just when he thought he'd worked it out, along came a new piece that didn't fit. Scott altered course and headed for Fish Creek.

The Commission had given the fishermen another day out, and aboard the *Nellie J* Vic and his crew were fitting out for the morning. Vic was bent over the engine wall, cussing and fuming, and most of the crew were working on the nets, trying to stay out of his way.

"Son of a bitch," Vic muttered, banging at the iron block with his big wrench.

"What's the matter?" Scott asked.

"The timing on these fuckin' injectors is shitty. Could quit on us right in the middle of a set."

"Probably needs to be reset in the shop." Jonesy, the pole man, spoke the obvious.

"Tell me what I don't know," Vic snapped. He tightened a lug, dropped the wrench to the deck, swearing, and climbed out of the well. "We'll have to run with them as they are."

"They sound fine to me," Georgie said cheerfully.

Vic glared at him. "What the hell do you know?"

Georgie shrugged and joined the others who were rewinding the spool.

As Scott had hoped, Vic had news about the ownership of the *Pilgrim*. "I talked to a gill-netter I know who operates out of Nainamo. He says the *Pilgrim* got bought up by a big conglomerate called Camstar, that they're buying up everything in sight."

"When did they buy the *Pilgrim*?"

"End of season three years ago."

"Is it a Canadian company?"

"He didn't know for sure, but said they were big shots. Multinationals is my guess, don't belong to any country. Gets them around the taxes." Vic grinned. "Tell you, Doc, I wish I could get so fuckin' smart."

"Your friend said they were buying up other properties?"

"Yeah—real estate, small businesses, fishing boats." The frown returned. "Bet they picked *them* up dirt cheap."

As a natural progression, Vic started in on the problems of the Canadian fishermen, which, apparently, were much the same as those for the Americans. Then Georgie bounced over with a report from one of the gill-netters that the sockeye run was in, and Vic cheered up like a newly lit candle. "Hey, Doc, wanna go out with us?"

Scott started to say yes, remembered Henry's party, and regretfully declined.

Vic laughed. "Next time maybe." Scott started for the Jeep, and Vic called after him, "By the way, Doc, on those blinking lights. Billy says to tell you it's definitely not the Indians."

Scott delivered Erin's groceries and the unwelcome news about Brice's visit.

"But he told me he couldn't possibly get away," she said with an unhappy face.

"That was before Leroy found out the mask was a fake, I imagine."

Al looked up from his typewriter. "Well? What did the big man say?"

"They're for real. I imagine Owen either got taken on one or he filled out his bedroom with a phony to make the walls come out even." Scott grinned, but Erin continued to look glum. "Better be going," Scott said, starting for the door.

"Wait, I haven't paid you for the groceries." She started counting out bills. "Comes to ten dollars and nine cents. I'm short a penny."

"I'll trust you." They were standing in the doorway, and he remembered about Henry's housewarming. Thinking it would cheer her, he invited her to go.

"I'm sorry, Scott. I already promised Preston."

If it had been anyone but Preston Fields. This wasn't totally true. He'd looked forward to taking her to the party. He'd turned Vic down for fishing, and now he had to go to Henry's party and endure Cynthia and Lorene. He couldn't very well not go or Erin would think she was the cause, and as foolish as it was, his pride wouldn't permit that.

Sixteen

Preston rumbled into Al's drive in his red Porsche. He stepped out, brushed off a pale-blue sports jacket, adjusted his tie, and sauntered confidently up to the door. After a moment, the door opened, and he went in. Scott waited by the window until he came out again, squiring Erin. She was dressed in a stunning green dress, low-cut. Her fair hair flowed evenly over the suntanned shoulders. To say she was a knockout would have been understating it. They were both laughing and looked like one of the television commercials for the beautiful people, Preston's dark head bent over hers. Preston held the door of the little car while Erin stepped in like she'd done it many times before. Preston got in the driver's side, and they drove off.

Disgusted, Scott left the window. He rummaged through his closet until he found his best gray jacket. It matched the charcoal slacks, he decided, but needed a press. He shook it, with little results. Sighing deeply, he selected a tie of bright blue and finished dressing. "I won't be late," he promised Dandy, walking slowly across the road to pick up Al. At eight o'clock the sun was still setting over the creek.

Al wore his familiar tweed jacket, but his deference to the occasion wouldn't go as far as a tie. He had on one of those western rings with a shoelace looped through it, and, in spite of himself, looked very sprightly.

Scott greeted the old man sourly. "I guess it's just you and me."

Al grunted an answer that said he hadn't approved Erin's

choice himself. We're like two crusty old bachelors, Scott thought unhappily as they trudged up the road the short distance to Henry's housewarming.

It was coming on dusk, and the air still smelled of wild strawberries and dried pine needles. Cars stuck out along the narrow gravel road all the way north and around to the creek.

"Looks like he asked every nitwit on the island," Al complained as they turned into Henry's drive and the loud brass sounds of the Island Jazz Band.

Henry's four acres stood on a windy point. Shaded by huge spruce and pine, it was constantly in the shadows on the roadside, and on the waterside looked out under a single fir to a sweeping view south to Goose Island and north up San Juan Channel. From deeper in the woods where Henry kept the kennel for his hunting dogs, one of his black Labs started to howl in tune to the shrill blasts of the trumpets. The wailing continued for a moment, followed by a sharp yelp, and then silence.

"They may be good duck hunters," Al said with a smile, "but they sure kick up a racket."

"They seemed to have stopped quickly enough."

"Roger saw to it."

Henry's hired man saw to everything.

Bright lanterns lit up the drive, tunneling a path through pines and madronas, at the end of which rose a series of gables and interconnecting roofs of burnt-red tile. White stucco and massive hand-carved oak doors framed the entry. Henry stood in the open doorway, immaculately dressed in a hand-tailored gray suit, white shirt, and bright red tie, looking prosperous and much younger than his eighty-two years. His appearance was in remarkable contrast to the way he normally looked walking the beach in the torn flannel shirt, baggy old suit-pant castoffs, zipper half down.

Henry Mason was a self-made millionaire who had, according to the stories, built his empire on hard work, shrewd manipulations, thrift, and distrust. He made his poke in Alaska, some said by unsavory means, and went into the loan business.

"He plays by the rules," Fred, who knew about such things, told Scott. "He picks companies where the book value is high enough to cover him, and he's a damn good judge of horseflesh. I can't remember anyone ever defaulting on old Henry." Fred grinned. "One wouldn't dare."

"You mean Henry's a loan shark?"

Fred laughed again. "If you ask him, he's just saving capital-starved small businesses when no one else will loan them a dime."

Henry had married and divorced three times. He'd sired no children from those marriages, and now, alone except for his hired man, Roger, he lived the life of a semirecluse. When he built Santana, curiosity ran high. The man who'd spent his life counting every nickel was now spending it like there was no tomorrow. Skilled workmen from Seattle ferried on and off the island, laying marble and wood floors, setting sunken tubs and select fir beams.

"I wonder," Scott said, looking around at the custom-made Spanish windows, "how the old boy bore up under all those cost overruns."

"Poorly," Al chuckled.

At the moment, Henry appeared to be holding up remarkably. "Doctor, glad you could come." His bony fingers gripped Scott's hand firmly. "Al tells me you were called in on Owen last week."

"Yes, that's right."

The eagle eyes flickered interest. "I ran into Brice Randall in town. He tells me one of Owen's artifacts was missing. How much do you imagine it was worth?"

"Don't know," Scott said, feeling Al's curious gaze.

The indifferent look Scott so often saw in the craggy face settled in again, and shortly Henry left to greet another guest.

"Mmmpf," Al muttered. "Was there some secret about the mask being a fake?"

"I was thinking of Erin and what Leroy said about keeping quiet what we know."

"Umm—see what you mean," Al said.

Al led the way through the entry hall into the dining room.

He remarked that the large turnout wasn't out of character for Henry. "What fun in having all that money if you can't flaunt it now and again?"

Like a heavy shadow, a big man in his fifties, dark-complexioned with sharply contrasting white hair shaved so short his brown scalp glistened under it, moved around them into the great hall. It was Roger.

"Man gives me the shivers," Al said. "Always slithering in and out. Henry's watchdog. Frankly, I'd sooner keep a Doberman."

There was a jam around the marble fountain at the far end of the room where pink champagne spouted in bubbling streams from the alabaster mouth of a child in a toga. In the room's center, the caterers had spread a lavish table, flown in from Seattle, oysters on the half-shell, tiny puff pastries filled with a smoked salmon mousse, crab legs, giant shrimp, slices of turkey and ham, and an endless assortment of salads, rolls, tarts, and pastries.

Al brightened at the sight of it. "This is more like it." He took an empty plate off the server and began busily filling it up.

Through the great hall to the terrace where the jazz combo played, Scott caught a glimpse of Erin. She and Preston were weaving and bending to the music and looking very pleased with each other. Scott wandered back to the fountain. The first person he brushed arms with was Millie. She was carrying a tray of dirty glasses to the kitchen. Scott stopped her to ask about Prissie.

Leroy had found her, she said. "She's home. That's the main thing. I guess the rest will take a little time." She forced a smile, but behind it there was pain and a disturbing hint of something Scott had not observed in Millie before. Millie wasn't a vindictive person, but clearly she bore a grudge against whoever had brought this trouble on her daughter.

The crowd around the fountain thickened. On the fringe of it, sipping a highball and leaning against the built-in server that filled up the west wall, was Fred, all by himself. "Don't worry," he said, reading Scott's mind, "they'll be back. They've just gone to the powder room. Ah, here they come now."

From the long hall, Cynthia and Lorene were squeezing

their way into the dining room. Lorene's mousy hair had more order to it than usual, puffed up and well lacquered. A rare trip to the local hairdresser, Scott guessed. Lorene looked determined. Cynthia, long, willowy, the auburn hair short and trimly brushed in soft waves, looked as she always looked—bored. Cynthia was attractive, but the vitality was definitely missing.

Cynthia was one of Lorene's oldest friends. They'd gone through private prep schools together and then to Vassar. Lorene left Vassar after her first year and transferred to the University of Washington where she met Fred. Cynthia stayed, graduated with a major in foreign languages, went on to graduate school in Georgetown, and married a member of the diplomatic corps. The marriage ended after two years. Cynthia returned to Seattle and moved casually from job to job with long periods of living the life of the idle rich, part of the time in her Seattle condo and part in the family house on the Cape. She'd been Lorene's pet project ever since.

"Here they are," Fred announced cheerfully as Lorene and Cynthia elbowed their way to Fred and Scott.

"Scottie," Lorene said in a scolding voice, "why didn't you call?"

Cynthia's smile lit up her face with a surprising release of energy. "Scott, nice to see you."

"How's the summer going?" Her answering laugh had new sparkle to it, usually pale cheeks bloomed with color, and, on second look, there was something different about Cynthia.

"I've been off the island," she said. "Just flew in for the weekend to catch old Henry's bash. Couldn't miss that."

"She's taken a job," Lorene said, as though she were describing a case of the measles.

"Good for you," Scott approved.

Cynthia flashed another smile. "I've opened my own travel agency. Seemed a shame to let all my experience go for naught. I work long hours, and I'm up to my eyes in clients, computers, and airline schedules. But do you know, Scottie, I love it. Can't wait to get back."

This was definitely a new Cynthia, and Scott had to start readjusting all his favorite clichés for the woman who'd always reminded him of the last leaf on the oak in winter. The transformation was heartening.

Lorene, however, wasn't at all pleased. She was like a possessive mother, reluctant to give up a daughter to an unwanted son-in-law. "That means you won't be here for the Windsure," Lorene said with a pout. "You know, we always go to Victoria for the races, and Scott's racing the *Picaroon* again this year."

Scott looked at Lorene in amazement.

"Are you, Scottie?" Cynthia asked.

"I haven't actually decided."

Feeling she was losing her cause, Lorene decided to retreat. "Talk to her, Scottie. Tell her she has to stay."

Fred shrugged and allowed Lorene to lead him away.

Cynthia laughed after them. "Don't mind Lorene. If she isn't directing someone's life, she just isn't happy."

"I know," Scott said with feeling.

"Still, it's good to see her firing again. I was worried about her last year."

"Oh, the trip to Switzerland?"

Cynthia nodded. "Her world fell apart all at once, losing her parents and the family fortune petering out."

This was something new.

"You didn't know about the bad investments? Swindle is really a better name for it. Come to think of it, I probably shouldn't be mentioning it. I don't think Fred knows the extent of the damage even now. Lorene's trust went under, too."

Scott felt a twinge of guilt, for he'd been going through the throes of the breakup at the time, and most likely Fred and Lorene had spared him their own problems. A wave of penitent forgiveness came over him. "Yes," he said. "Good to see her doing well." The sad moment passed. "Now, tell me about this budding business of yours."

It was all the encouragement she needed. She was more animated than he'd ever seen her, talking about travel snafus, tours, customers who wanted individual service. It was quickly clear that Cynthia, who'd always been directionless, had at last discovered what she wanted from life. Scott was frankly envious.

Al walked into the conversation. He'd always wanted to visit Europe and the Greek Isles, he said. That he'd never done so surprised Scott, who'd always thought him well traveled. Scott left the two of them huddled around the server in a lively discussion about tombs, cathedrals, and ruins.

Scott had never been comfortable with Toni's store parties. A most singular-minded group, store executives. As a consequence, he'd learned the solo art of circulating, which amounted to hanging on to the periphery of conversations, nodding owlishly, smiling appropriately, and moving on.

When Scott rejoined Cynthia and Al, Fred and Lorene were back. The room was densely packed, and someone bumped arms with Cynthia and spilled a few drops of champagne on her dress. Scott suggested a tour of the house would be safer.

The second part of Santana was as Scott had envisioned— sculptures and murals on white walls, but no trinkets or memorabilia, nothing personal. Here he missed Erin's insights, wondered what she thought of the strange mix of stone, marble, and concrete.

Fred admired the swimming pool, an inside-outside job with a sliding roof, now closed, and doors that opened onto the terrace. He stood on the pool's tiled edge, flexed his arms, and poised for a racing dive, just as he had in their college days when he'd been captain of the swim team. The smells of salt vapor and chlorine were almost overpowering, and the women started to look a little wilted.

Lorene complained that the steam was taking the curl out of her hair, and they left.

On the upper terrace the band played a lively rendition of "Sugar Blues," and several couples danced on the smooth stone tiles. In the far corner a bar had been set up, and two barmaids in black tights and silky bare-backed tops worked feverishly to keep up with the orders.

Fred and Lorene took to the dance floor and went at it, as they did everything, with a good deal of energy, swinging shoulders and hips. Scott looked at Cynthia, feeling an uncomfortable sensation in the pit of his stomach. "Want to try?"

Cynthia laughed. "I'm content to watch, if you are."

"A drink, then?" he asked."

"Seven-Up. Got an early day tomorrow."

Scott shouldered his way to the bar, ordered the drinks, returned with them, and found Cynthia enjoying the view from the terrace. The water was all in darkness, and the moon was settling over the Pass.

It had been hot in the dining room, but out here a breeze rustled off the water and cooled things down pleasantly. Just below, in the glow of the lower terrace lights, two people shared the moon. No mistaking the golden hair or the slim bronzed shoulders. It was Erin with Preston. A memory flashed painfully. Scott looked quickly away.

"What a lovely spot," Cynthia said, sitting down on the stone bench beside a big tree.

He settled down beside her. "Oh, yes—nice."

"How has it been going for you, Scottie?"

"Fine."

She sensed the change in him. "Do you still miss her terribly?"

It was so far from his thoughts and so unlike her to speak of Toni, it surprised him. Yet when he thought of it, from Cynthia, who'd known him through the difficult times, the question seemed natural and caused him none of the old distress. "I don't know if it's that. I'd like to understand."

"And you don't?"

"Not entirely."

Cynthia nodded, and for a moment he had the feeling she wanted to say something but didn't quite know how. The look went away, and she said, "I had a feeling you were different, that you weren't suffering anymore."

Suddenly he realized how it must have been for her, putting

up with his moods, not peppering him with questions. "And you, my dear Cyn, are different, too." The warmth and openness, misery shared, not held in. Yes, she was different.

She grasped his hand and held it. "We are a pair, aren't we? I've managed to get my life back together. God knows, it took long enough. Anyway, I know what it is to flounder, to need something and not have it." She looked away, and her color deepened. "I want you to know if you ever need a shoulder to cry on, I'm always available."

He knew what she was offering. They were alike in many ways, private and often lonely people. He kissed her softly on the cheek. "I appreciate that, Cyn. I do."

She laughed shyly. "You have always been a true friend."

He was afraid it wasn't true. He thought back to the times he'd worked so assiduously to avoid Lorene's arrangements. But apparently Cynthia hadn't known, or if she had, she'd understood, and there'd always been the mutual respect. If he came away from the evening with nothing else, this understanding between two old friends was worth it all.

On the dance floor the couples were still swinging to the music of the Island Jazz, but something new had been added. "Don't look now," Scott said, "but isn't that Marilyn Delaney dancing with Fred?"

Cynthia nodded, not smiling. "And if you could see Lorene's face."

Such a dark look! Scott guessed the reason. Marilyn, who'd had a great deal too much to drink, was draped around Fred, and they were shuffling around the floor to the fast tempo of the drums and putting on quite a show. The crowd from the bar began collecting near the dance floor to watch. Prominent among them was Bob Delaney, who, for a change, appeared sober and, like Lorene, was none too happy. Fred threw Marilyn into a spin, retrieved her before she fell. Marilyn's laughter trilled across the room.

Scott figured Fred could handle the situation, but Cynthia was worried, and breathed a sigh of relief when the number ended and Fred returned Marilyn to her husband.

"Don't worry about Fred. He enjoys being the life of the party."

"It's not Fred I'm worried about."

Scott followed the direction of Cynthia's gaze to Lorene, who was still glowering at Fred. Fred beat a dutiful path back to her side.

Scott chuckled. "She'll get over it."

But Bob showed no signs of getting over it. He grabbed Marilyn by the wrist and pulled her to the doorway. "You need air."

"I don't," she protested, slipping from his grasp and almost falling again.

He got another hold on her. They scuffled, and everyone pretended not to notice as Bob half led and half dragged his wife toward the hall. "You're going home!" he said, the veins pulsating in his temples.

Lorene thought it terrible how some people couldn't hold their liquor. Al said Marilyn had been talking wild all evening about blinking lights and fishing boats and all sorts of nonsense. "Did the right thing taking her home."

"Mmm," Fred said.

From the shadows of the giant fir, Henry's man Roger watched and said nothing.

Shortly, Cynthia said she had to go—a late flight, morning appointments.

"I'll drive you to the airport," Scott offered.

Cynthia smiled and shook her head. "Lorene's taking me after she drops Fred off. Women talk, you know. But don't forget, Scottie, the standing invitation."

Beside him, Al lifted a curious eyebrow, and Scott waved good-bye to Cynthia.

Seventeen

The happy mood of Henry's turned to tragedy before the coming of the morning tide. It was shortly after two, and the party was still going strong. During music breaks from Santana, from his bed Scott heard occasional bursts of laughter pealing down the beach.

Scott lay there, between snatches of semiconsciousness, dimly aware of the brass sounds from the Island Jazz trumpeting sweetly across the water. The music ended abruptly with a clarinet note and the jangled empty noises of trumpets and reeds being blown clean for packing back into their cases. Laughter and talk drifted louder from the beach, the unmistakable sign that Henry's party was finally breaking up.

From the driftwood, a crane squawked noisily and with rustling of heavy wings, took flight. A distant wail followed, not a living sound. Scott felt displaced, as though he were somewhere else. His immediate sense was of standing in the OR at the hospital while they wheeled in a victim of an accident on the freeway. The operating-room lights blazed. He was gowned, waiting for anesthesia to confirm the patient was under.

The wail turned to a shriek, and Dandy started to howl. Coming fully awake, Scott shot up and padded barefoot to the window. Across Cattle Pass the lights blinked steadily. From the road, an engine rumbled, and tires scraped over gravel and thudded to a stop. Dandy's howl turned to a sharp bark, and Scott realized someone was pounding on the door. It was Leroy's deputy, Harold, and from his face Scott knew right away there was big trouble.

"There's been another shooting. Can you come quick?"

For one long petrifying second, Scott knew fear. "Who?" he said, his voice breaking above a whisper.

Harold looked like he was going to be sick. "Marilyn Delaney—another shotgun blast. Leroy says she's dead."

"I'll just get some clothes on."

They drove the short distance to the Delaney cottage at full speed and with the blue lights flashing. Outside the rustic cedar cabin, Pauline and Craig Deekins and Jerry Butler, who'd been part of the Delaney party earlier, hovered under the dim lights of the lamppost. Anxiety was written all over their faces.

"How is she?" Craig asked in a husky voice, his eyes resembling the hollow rings of an owl in the semidarkness.

"We—we only just heard," Pauline whispered. "Someone said she was dead."

Across the road a dog barked. This was followed by the echoing yelps from Henry's hunting hounds several hundred yards away.

Scott followed Harold through the front door directly into the living room, and there she was, dressed in a short sheer nightgown, a gaping wound in her chest. Marilyn had always been well filled out, but she was much thinner and smaller in death. She lay crumpled on her back on the carpet, much as Owen had lain only a few days earlier. The room smelled strongly of bourbon, and it all worked to give Scott an overpowering feeling of déjà vu, the nasty hole that had blown her breast and neck open, the bulging eyes that stared sightless at the ceiling. Harold took one look and shot for the door.

"Where's Bob?"

Leroy pointed to the kitchen where Bob sat slumped over the table, his head buried in his arms, an untouched tumbler of bourbon in front of him. Another of Leroy's men stood guard over him, but there was no need. Bob wasn't going anywhere. He didn't even look up.

"Shotgun again."

Leroy nodded.

"Who reported it?"

Leroy pointed at Bob. "He called a few minutes ago. Said he'd gone for a walk and when he returned he found her that way."

"Then he didn't hear the shot?"

"So he says."

"I doubt anyone could have over the noise of the Island Jazz."

"Except Bob." Leroy's mouth was set grimly.

"You don't think *Bob* did it?"

Leroy didn't answer. "I wonder, could you fix a time of death?"

"It was after eleven. That's when Marilyn left the party."

"Leaves a lot of time in between."

Scott touched Marilyn's arm. It was cool and firm. "An hour is my guess."

Leroy glanced into the kitchen. Bob hadn't moved. Leroy lowered his voice to a whisper. "You saw her at the party at eleven?"

"Yes, and so did everyone else," Scott whispered back.

"I understand she had too much to drink."

The smell of liquor in the room was something of a giveaway. Scott nodded.

"How long did the party last?"

"It just broke up a few minutes ago."

Leroy rubbed his chin thoughtfully. "She left pretty early. Did she pass out, have to be carried home? Something like that?"

"She was walking when I last saw her."

"Any arguments?"

Scott shrugged. "Not really." He repeated the scene between Marilyn and Bob.

"Did he shove her around?"

"No—nothing like that. She was a little unsteady on her

feet, and I imagine he wanted to get her out of there before she passed out. That's all there was to it."

Leroy wrote on his notepad.

"Where's the coroner?"

"He's on his way."

Harold, still ghostly pale, stuck his head in the door. "Lotta people collecting here. What should I do about them?"

"Anyone know anything?"

"They say not."

"Unless you find someone who knows anything, tell them to go on home."

"What about Kenny?"

"What about him?"

"He says he has a deadline."

With public image a concern for Leroy at this point, the reporter from the local paper was a little harder to put off. Leroy sighed heavily. "Okay, tell him to wait a minute."

Harold nodded and backed out.

Around the rooms all else appeared normal. It was a small cabin with a living room that opened into the kitchen, a single bedroom, and bath. The Delaneys had been renting it summers for the past three years from the owners, who were from off-island and using the place for a tax write-off. It was designed for two people, which was no problem for the Delaneys, who had only one grown son from Bob's previous marriage.

Bright watercolors hung on the walls, and white tie-back curtains, crisp and neat, framed the big windows, giving the room a cheerful look. Erin would approve. Scott looked across at Leroy, suddenly feeling very tired.

"Well, Doc?"

Dutifully, Scott bent over Marilyn's body again, studied for a moment the way one leg was bent under the other. From here, his eyes traced a slow pattern to the chest and neck.

"What is it?" Leroy said. "Something crazy. I can see it in your face."

"See this little red mark on her throat, like a bruise, above the wound?"

Leroy dropped to his knees and inspected the barely visible spot.

"Now look at the wound itself."

Leroy concentrated on the hole in her chest. "Uh-huh."

"There's not enough blood. It's not red and oozing like it ought to be. I don't know what the coroner will say, but my guess is she was strangled to death."

"Killed twice?"

"In a manner of speaking."

Leroy wiped sweat from his forehead with his sleeve. "What do you think was used?"

"A silk stocking, something like that."

"Take someone strong?"

"Not in Marilyn's condition."

Noise from the kitchen distracted them. Bob was weeping. He looked up for a moment, his face ash-white and full of pain. Scott knew the look. He'd seen it in his own mirror not many months ago. Yet, as things stood, it didn't look at all good for Bob Delaney.

Frank Gilly, funeral director and *pro tem* coroner for the island, arrived in his usual breathless state. He saw Marilyn and shook his head. "Needs an autopsy. Better get her to Mt. Vernon. Can't do much here."

"I don't think you need me anymore," Scott said.

Leroy looked up, distracted. "Thanks for coming, Doc. Oh, when you go out, would you tell Kenny to come on in?"

Scott stepped out into the cool dampness of the predawn morning and sucked in a giant breath of air, inhaled the sweet smells of dew-soaked fir needles, and felt much better. He delivered his message to Kenny, who rushed past and banged into the house. Scott reminded himself that Kenny probably hadn't known Marilyn. To him, she was just a story, and on the small island newspaper, perhaps the biggest story of Kenny's career. How could he be expected to care? The Seattle reporters would be next. May as well get used to it.

In spite of Harold, a much larger crowd now gathered on the road outside the cottage. The presence of the coroner's wagon told them all they needed to know, but they stayed anyway, as though expecting more. Some were still dressed in their party clothes; a few were in pajamas and robes.

The front door of the cottage opened, and Bob stepped out, followed by the deputy. Bob's face and eyes were red and swollen, and his mouth grimly shut. He walked by them, not looking or talking, even to his friends. He piled into the patrol car, and the door shut on his grieving face. The chatter grew, the predictable speculations about how Marilyn died. Bob was an easy answer, one most probably accepted. But there were doubts, the doubts raised by the specter of Owen.

When Owen died everyone had been shocked, but not particularly sorry. Even from those who'd attended his parties one received no feeling of remorse about Owen. It was as if his death were somehow earned, a result of the way he lived. Marilyn was quite different. Who could find a reason for it? She drank too much, talked too much, and raced her cars and the boat too fast, but she wasn't the sort of person who generated hate, who aroused the kind of malice that provokes murder. If her husband hadn't killed her, that meant a deranged and dangerous killer was loose, a killer who might strike again, and Scott knew it was this idea that was bringing fear to them all.

The door opened again, and Frank wheeled out Marilyn's draped body. There was a low moan across the grass. Leroy banged out behind and stood guard by his patrol wagon while they shoved the stretcher into Frank's van. Leroy turned to Scott. "I'm leaving one of my deputies to watch the place." Then he climbed into his wagon and stuck his head out the window. "Go on home," he told the crowd. "You're no help here."

The revolving lights on both vehicles flashed through the big branches of the firs, a depressing reminder of what had called them to this peaceful spot. Everyone moved back slowly; a few already drifted down the road to their homes, heads bowed in depressed silence. Scott started to follow, and a dark form walked uncertainly toward him.

"Scottie, that you?"

"Fred?"

"Yeah. My God, what's going on? Lorene came back from the airport and said she saw the sheriff's wagon go by flashing his lights. I sent her to bed and decided to run up and see what was going on. Ran into Henry's man, Roger. He said Marilyn had been shot, just like Owen. Is it true?"

Scott nodded. "Afraid it is."

Fred sagged against a tree, shaking his head. "Only a couple of hours ago we were dancing, and she was having a helluva time. Oh, shit! We got a madman running loose around here, do you know that?"

"Yes," Scott said grimly, "and I hope Leroy gets a handle on it soon."

Fred drew in his breath sharply. "You think he'll kill again?"

"Seems a strong possibility, don't you think?"

Fred's face froze, and Scott imagined he was thinking of Lorene, alone. "I'll talk to you later," he said, starting for home at a trot.

The lights were on in Al's house. Al was still in his pajamas. Erin had thrown a robe over her nightgown. She wore no makeup, but she was wide awake and clearly apprehensive.

"Siren woke us," Al said. "Then Henry called, all shook up. He said he'd heard somebody shot Marilyn Delaney." Al studied Scott's face. "I can see it's all true."

Scott nodded glumly. "She's dead."

"Oh, no," Erin said. "We'd so hoped . . . poor Marilyn." She sank into Al's big chair, looking lost in it. How vulnerable she was, Scott thought.

He touched her hand. "How about some coffee?"

Erin made the coffee and they sat, staring into the mugs,

and tried to puzzle out the strange circumstances of Marilyn's death.

Erin thought Bob cared too much for his wife to have done it.

"What's that got to do with it?" Al sniffed. "You'd be surprised what goes on in families. I heard a statistic the other day about the number of husbands and wives who get into rows that end in a shooting. Marilyn probably mouthed off, and Bob let her have it, simple as that."

"That doesn't explain Owen's death, and Marilyn was killed the same way."

"Not quite." Scott told them about the strangling.

Erin paled, and Al stuck his pipe tightly between his teeth.

"You do think the murders are connected?" Erin said.

"I'm afraid I do."

They fell silent.

"We have to do something," Erin said, breaking the silence.

"Do what?" Al snapped.

"I don't know, but we can't just sit around while some mad person goes after us, one by one."

"You're overdramatizing it," Al said in a voice that lacked conviction.

"Am I? Two dead, three, if you count the person found off South Beach, and Prissie's missing."

Scott smiled. Good news on that, at least. "The sheriff found her. I talked to Millie at the party. She's home, and she's all right." He didn't think the lie would harm anyone. Prissie was a long way from all right.

Erin looked much relieved. "But you haven't said anything about the killings. Don't you agree this person is crazed?"

"I think 'crazed' is the wrong word."

"Don't you think strangling someone and then shooting them with a shotgun is crazed?"

"Panicked, maybe. No, there's a pattern here that is entirely too rational to be put off to mere madness. Do you see?"

"I suppose, but isn't there anything we can do?"

"Yes—I think there is."

They both perked up.

"It would mean going off the island."

Erin brightened. "Where?"

"Campbell River."

The smile spread across her face. "Why did I know you were going to say that?"

"When do we start?" Al asked, appearing to read Scott's fears.

"How about catching the noon ferry today?"

"I'll call Paul, have him look in on the animals," Al said.

"We might be staying a couple of days," Scott told Erin. "You'll want to take some warm clothes. It can get cold up there, and we'll be going for a boat ride."

Eighteen

A warm south wind blew off Cape Mudge at the passage to Campbell River, stirring up a wild sea. It was hot and dusty as Scott drew up in front of Discovery Inn. The inn stood on the quay overlooking the breakwater. Only a few paces away a small car ferry ran the twenty-minute hop to Quadra, the largest island in the Discovery Island chain. It was from Quadra Scott hoped to set out in the morning.

Now, at midday, he wanted to spend the afternoon following a hunch. The problem at the moment was Al. The long drive from Sidney had proved an ordeal after a night with little sleep, and he was clearly out of sorts. He piled out of the Jeep, looking tired and complaining of a backache.

They checked into the inn, and over lunch Scott suggested Al see what he could learn from the local library while Scott and Erin covered the real estate offices. It was a move designed more to take the pressure off him than out of any hope they'd find anything.

"We can meet back here for dinner and compare notes. How does that suit you, Al?"

The professor, who'd logged more hours in reference rooms than most had in classrooms, pounced on the idea. "Can't see what you hope to learn from a bunch of real estate agents."

"Probably nothing. All I know is Delaney got a good case of the shakes every time Marilyn mentioned Campbell River. I have to wonder why."

Campbell River, a hundred miles north of Victoria, sat at the northwestern end of the Strait of Georgia not far from Kelsey Bay, the jumping-off place for the Inside Passage to Alaska. Unlike in Victoria, one saw few men in three-piece suits in Campbell River. This was the home of the Tyee salmon, the land of hobnailed boots, wind slickers, and heavy Cowichan sweaters.

Scott had sailed here in his college days, poked around the hundreds of tiny islands that shaped the narrow waterways in this northern chain, and remembered unpredictable storms, fierce tidal rips, dense forests, and rocky beaches. He found himself excited at the prospect of probing again the tiny coves, arms, and inlets. Tomorrow they would do that when they began their search for the *Pilgrim*. Vic said she'd been spotted around Read and Cortes, so that's where they'd look. It might all be for nothing, but Scott didn't mind.

"Where do we begin our sleuthing?" Erin asked.

"We start by walking."

"I hate to ring a sour note, but isn't it a little hard when we don't know what we're looking for?"

"We're looking for something bizarre."

"I should have guessed."

With that, they set out.

The real estate offices hummed with their Apples and IBMs. The salespeople were friendly and looked to their computer screens for listings such as Scott described. The computers spit out ranchettes, river lots, and farms, all pretty normal stuff. Scott looked at maps and pictures of view property and forested acreage, and in none of it did he see anything out of the way or connected to American real estate interests. After a half-dozen realtors, it began to appear Al had been right about the futility of this task.

After walking for most of two hours, they found themselves back on the quay. Erin looked longingly across the parking lot at the hotel. Scott gave her hand an encouraging squeeze. "Shall we just try that little office there by the marina and then call it a day?"

The windows of the Donald Miller Real Estate Agency were almost totally obscured by pictures of houses and waterfront properties. Inside was little different. In contrast to the computer-run offices they'd been in, it lacked any kind of filing system whatsoever. Plot plans, pictures, and real estate listings, printed and mimeographed, were piled atop the desk, tables, and chairs, so there wasn't a clear space anywhere. On the walls were a series of dusty-framed aerial shots of the islands and a giant map of the region. The only concession to the computer age here was a small copying machine that sat half hidden by the papers.

Miller, a slight-boned man with bright red cheeks, rose from behind the manila folders, shifted papers around until he'd cleared two chairs, and invited them to sit down. It became quickly clear why he didn't need the computers. He kept his listings firmly filed in his head.

He hummed happily as he thumbed through his folders. "Yes—yes, we have some nice pieces. Might be just what you're looking for. Yes, here it is." He pulled one folder from the stack. "A lovely one. A hundred acres on the river. Only twelve miles inland." He slipped an aerial photograph of a large tract of land with a dense stand of firs and a wide stretch of river from the file and laid it in front of them.

"Interesting," Scott said. "How much?"

Here Miller turned cagy. "You may have heard real estate is depressed in this area. This parcel would normally sell for four or five hundred thousand, but with the American dollar difference and the market being down, I think you might pick it up for half that. Can't guarantee it, but I think the owners would entertain a reasonable offer."

"Do you have anything closer to Gold River?"

Miller's smile wavered. "You won't do as well in that direction."

Scott's interest picked up. "Why? I thought the mines were shut down."

"Not entirely." Miller doodled with his pencil on the notepad in front of him. "There's been some American interest over there. Upped the prices."

Beside Scott, Erin drew in her breath softly.

"Oddest thing, I haven't the least idea what's causing it. I imagine it's speculation with future mining in mind, but I must say there's more potential for new deposits in the river piece I've showed you."

"*Very* odd," Erin said, with a meaningful glance at Scott. "Where is this property?"

Miller walked over to the map on the wall and traced a line with his finger. "South and just a little east of Gold River."

"And you've had a number of sales there?"

"I haven't, no. This is an exclusive run by a large combine. I believe it's what you call a REIT."

"A Real Estate Investment Trust?"

"Yes. This company calls itself Stark, or something of the sort. I know of one section they've sold and resold three times in the past twelve months, and each time the price doubled, and the same company carried the paper for all of it. Much of it, of course, is stock sales." He shrugged. "At least, so I've heard."

"Sounds like they struck gold," Erin said.

"Not according to our local geologists. No, it's my opinion they've done an overly creative selling job."

"A fraud?"

Miller smiled. "Those wouldn't be my words, but I think you have the idea. I like to warn Americans, but in most cases the sales occur from the States' side, and the people never see the property."

"That's the whole idea of a REIT, isn't it?" Erin said. "To place trust in a company that knows where good buys can be found?"

"Yes, but here the prices are much too high. The worst part for us, it artificially raises land values in that area."

Scott promised to call Miller back, and they left the realtor's office. On the street, Erin puzzled over their findings. "I can feel we're getting close, but what does it all mean?"

They slipped into the marina and arranged for a twenty-two-foot Whaler Revenge that had a roomy cockpit with pedestal chairs for the pilot and the passenger and storage under the bow. Erin lifted an eyebrow at the price, but Scott pointed out they knew firsthand it was a fast boat and maneuverable, and with the two-hundred-horsepower Mercury outboard engine, just what they needed if they were going to cover a long distance in a hurry. He paid the deposit, and they left.

It was four when Scott left Erin at her room with plans to meet in the lounge for drinks at six. Just enough time to do what he had to do.

In the town hall the clerk kept all the records of sales and transfers of title, but couldn't help without a code number to feed into the computer. The clerk asked if he had thought of checking with title insurance.

Scott went directly to the offices of the title insurance company. "I am considering purchasing a large tract, and I'd like to be certain the title is clear," Scott told the man in charge.

The man looked back, bewildered. "That is why you buy title insurance."

"True, but I represent a consortium, you see, and my people like to be sure they're dealing with a reputable company."

The agent poked a pencil at his chin. "I don't see how I can help."

"Can you tell me if you've handled sales for a company called Camstar?"

"I don't recall that name."

"They could go by another—Stark, something like that."

He thought a moment. "You wouldn't by chance mean Star Limited?"

"I think that is just what I mean," Scott said, with effort not sounding too excited.

"You don't need to worry about them. They're part of a conglomerate based in Ottawa, heavily capitalized."

"Would any of their properties be recorded in the town records?"

"Ask the town clerk to show you the Gold River additions M-6705. Star has been a prime mover of that property."

"I'd heard the mines were mostly out of production now."

"That isn't actually mine property." He winked knowingly. "Tax credits. Not good for much else."

In the town hall, Scott struck a silver lode of his own. It

turned up on the computer names, dates, sales, and Owen, listed as the company's officer of record. It confirmed Delaney's connection to Owen, but left unexplained what they were doing with the property and how they were selling it at such big markups. Had they struck gold, as Erin had suggested? If so, why the resales? And who was successor to Owen?

Nothing in it refuted Scott's original hunch. Still, he needed at least one or two more pieces of information to complete the puzzle. One thing was grimly clear. The mere mention of this connection brought poor Marilyn a ghastly death, and now both he and Erin undoubtedly knew as much as she.

Vacationers filled up the cocktail lounge where Scott waited for Al and Erin. They arrived with Erin, looking fresh and unaware of danger in any form. He vowed to keep it that way. He also decided he wouldn't tell them about the trip to the town hall, which could only increase their exposure to risk.

"Incredible library they have here," Al said.

"Find anything?"

"Didn't have enough time." Al had decided he didn't want to run the boat trip around Quadra in the morning.

"We know the *Pilgrim's* running in these waters, Al," Scott argued. "It's not a complete waste."

"What do you hope to learn if you find her?"

"How she operates. If she is what she claims to be, a researcher for the experimental lab."

"And if she isn't, what then? You could find a peck of trouble."

Scott laughed. "They're just students, Al. Anyway, we don't plan on getting that close."

"And if you don't find her?"

"We'll have a nice run in the islands. Doesn't that tempt you?"

"Not one little bit."

Nineteen

The Whaler cut a clean path across the channel toward Cape Mudge and the southern tip of Quadra Island. From Campbell River there were two passages to the north. One went through the swift waters of Seymour Narrows, where the peaks of Ripple Rock, since blasted out, had once made this a graveyard for ships. The other, around Cape Mudge with its exposure to strong southerly winds, went through the channels and arms that filled the waterways all the way north to Johnstone Strait. Scott took this heading and within ten minutes closed in on Cape Mudge and the Indian carvings. Grim faces carved into the granite boulders stuck out along the tidal flats, the curious remains of the early Indians.

"Like the African masks," Erin said.

"Petroglyphs. Date back to prehistoric times. Spirit beings to ward off storms and marauding tribes."

"Somber."

As they rounded the point, a dragon's head with the sharp fangs of a wolf protruded ominously from the tide flat. Erin shivered, and for a moment Scott had a second thought about their quest. He turned into the ice-blue waters of Sutil Channel. A peaceful flock of gulls flew over, and the feeling passed.

He raced toward Read, where he hoped they might find the *Pilgrim*. It had been years since he'd cruised these islands, but he remembered the rocks and swift current and logs that broke free of their booms from nearby logging operations. He reminded himself to keep an eye out for deadheads, those half-submerged logs so deadly to props and hulls.

Erin caught the idea and gave up the comfort of the cushioned chair to stand beside him. She gripped the cockpit rail and scanned the water ahead. "I'll be lookout."

Off to the north, a needle-shaped cloud marred the blue sky, and Scott had another memory of the squalls that came up with some frequency in these waters. In a way this was one of the fascinating parts of the northern islands. Storms rolled in off the strait without warning. The north part of the chain—Sonora, Stuart, and Thurlow—was, in fact, much like a rainbelt, with overcast weather a good part of the time, undoubtedly one reason these islands remained the most uninhabited of them all. The Whaler scooted past Quadra's small marina at Rebecca Spit, where a flotilla of pleasure boats sat tied to the floats. From here on marinas and gas docks would fall few and far between, and they'd have to check their fuel carefully.

"We'll try Read first," he said.

Read Island hung directly west of Quadra and meandered north. Despite its proximity to Quadra and a history of early exploration and settlement, few families lived here, and abandoned homesteads scattered along its backwood roads. There were good anchorages around the island, most still in their natural state of seclusion and tranquility. Expecting to find the big schooner in one isolated anchorage among hundreds was a little like trying to find one tree in a forest. But Scott counted heavily on Vic's information, and, according to Vic, the *Pilgrim* had been sighted several times around Read and Cortes. This might mean they had a regular run between the two islands, and this narrowed the field of search considerably.

They ran the open waters for only a few minutes before they reached the coves and pockets along Read's southern banks. Scott eased the throttle, and they started through what first appeared to be a narrow passageway. Oyster catchers and terns fluttered into the air in a thick cloud of black and gray. The water rippled all the way across the shallow inlet. The low-pitched *kee-er* of a single gull cried out in protest.

"A lagoon!" Erin said.

It was a tidal backwash, overgrown with trees and ferns that dropped between large boulders right to the water's edge. Scott lowered their speed again, and they cut a slow trail through the still waters. Running close to shore they could reach out and touch the twisted boughs of firs and elms with their fingers.

From the lagoon, they broke out into the open again and came upon a trio of cabin cruisers traveling together. They ran alongside the small boats, all churning up white foaming tails. A cluster of tiny islands stretched out ahead of them. The cruisers angled off on a southeasterly heading toward Cortes. Erin waved and received answering waves, and their fellow wanderers quickly put distance between them. Scott continued north.

"We'll swing into Evans Bay. We can gas up at Government dock and go on. There's a little inlet up there; might be a nice stop for lunch."

Erin nodded contentment with the plan, and in this pleasant fashion they cruised on, most of the time at trolling speed, pausing to drop into an intriguing cove here and there and not giving much thought to their intended purpose.

There were only a few boats at Evans Bay, and they had no waiting time at the gas dock. The Whaler took twenty gallons, which meant the big Mercury engine had used half a tank. By Scott's calculations they had four hours' running time to find the *Pilgrim* before they would need to fill up again.

It was eleven-thirty when they found the place Scott had in mind for lunch, a small nook behind Frederic Point, completely walled in on all sides by grassy banks and trees, with a generous stretch of sand beach. They stuffed their gear into the backpack and dropped over the side into ankle-high water. They waded ashore, slipping and stumbling barefoot over the slime-green pebbles. The water was surprisingly warm. Like many of the protected coves in summer, the sun had baked in here, so there was a greenhouse effect on the water and plants.

"I wish I'd brought my swimsuit," Erin said.

"Swim as you are," Scott suggested. "I won't mind."

Erin laughed at the idea and found a sandy mound in front of a clump of driftwood that she quickly declared an ideal spot for their picnic. Scott secured the bowline to a rock and Erin laid out the beach towel.

She apportioned the contents of the lunch and Scott opened a bottle of wine, and they dug their bare toes into the warm sand and spent the next half hour conjecturing about the *Pilgrim*. Scott still thought it too much ship for students. Erin argued it was a wonderful training experience for them. Maybe that was the idea.

After lunch they took up their course again along the shoal passageway into Evans Bay. It was Scott's intention to run up the arm beyond Bird Cove, and if they didn't sight the *Pilgrim* in short order to run across to Cortes, where they could refuel and return to Campbell River. It wasn't much of a plan, but with what he knew about the anchorages in this area, it was the best he could come up with.

"How close are we to Bird Cove?"

"Not far."

Across to the north the needle-shaped cloud had ballooned into a whale.

"Anything wrong?"

"No. We could get a change in weather. Might have to cut it short. Might have to give up Cortes altogether."

Scott increased their speed and pondered the shorelines with new doubts. It was like running through an eight-foot-high maze of hedgerows, impossible to see the opening to one cove until you were fully upon it, each arm hiding the next. He glanced at the gas gauge and knew they had time and fuel to check only a few.

Bird Cove was a small, shallow anchorage. Scott shook his head. "Not enough draught for her here."

It was as he'd thought. If she were here at all, she'd undoubtedly gone up one of the long arms. But which, the one that veered west or the one that turned east, miles deep and wild? The shadows lengthened on the water, and all across Sutil Channel to Cortes the sea turned from sapphire-blue to a dark turquoise, sending definite signals of a coming turn in the weather.

Scott chose the east arm, thinking it the most protected and the most likely to have deep enough waters for a ship of the *Pilgrim's* size. The inlet had a number of bends and turns, and in most there was no sign anyone living had ever set foot on her before. There weren't even traces of logging trails or abandoned pastures, nothing except trees, moss, and rocks.

"Gives you a strange feeling," Erin said, and he wondered if the thought had hit her, too, that coming upon the *Pilgrim* in such a remote place might not be such a good idea after all.

Until now it had been a warm run, the only wind coming from their own movement through the quiet waters. All at once a small breeze sent a quiver over the water, and with it, cooler air. There wasn't much time left for their exploring. "Just a couple more turns. She twists in here."

They came upon it almost by accident. It looked like a long jetty, but when they turned into it, they found a deep cove with thick stands of firs, spruce, pine, and oak growing from the water's bank, backed by a steep rise of land, also densely covered with trees. Scott throttled down. They coasted around another bend, and there she was, looking like an oversize dolphin in a backyard swimming pool: the long cutter bow, the three tall masts, sails fastened to her rails, the Maple Leaf hanging limp from her mizzen gaff, lying at anchor, peaceful as a child at sleep. It was the *Pilgrim*.

"Fantastic," Erin murmured.

He had only half expected to find her, and at least thought to come upon her from a distance, just in case those two were on board. Stumbling on her this way, up so close they could see the scuff marks on her rails and the rust stains on her canvas, and no place to run without being seen, concerns ran through his head. Marilyn's murder led him to believe the two men called Charlie and Jerry were either still hiding somewhere on San Juan Island or headed for parts unknown, but what if his hunch they were tied in with the *Pilgrim* was right and they'd sought refuge here?

It was a stupid time for such thoughts. His instincts told him he'd better cut and run. But they'd come a long way, and there was no good reason for such fears. They couldn't observe the big ship from afar as he'd planned, but if they took reasonable precautions, they could avert a confrontation. They drifted quietly back into the cove, slipped around the schooner from her stern. Nothing moved, and Scott began to breathe more normally. "Hello, there!"

There was only the sound of a wavelet from the Whaler's wake slapping gently against the sides of the ship. "Anyone aboard?" Still no answer.

Scott tried to think how they would operate. Go out in skiffs to gather samples, with faculty or without. Scott brought the Whaler alongside and tied a line on her starboard cleat. A rope ladder hung over the gunwale as though it had been recently used, and there was only one skiff on her decks.

"Looks like they've gone ashore," Scott said. "I'll have a quick peek. Give a whistle if you see anything."

Erin nodded. "Don't be long." The quiver in her voice said she shared his concerns.

He killed the engine and left her with her eyes firmly fixed on the shore. "I'll be right back."

The cabin door was open, which indicated either trust in the remoteness of their anchorage or that the residents would soon be back. Opting to suspect the former, Scott leaned over the well. "Hello, there!" Above him, the boom creaked as it shifted, stirred by the Whaler's wake. All clear. Scott started down the gangway, confirmed almost immediately that no one was aboard, and instantly felt better. It was a roomy cabin with bunks forward and aft, and a galley and lounge in the center. The smell of morning bacon was trapped in with the musty odor of wet wood. Wet wood was not uncommon in old boats, and pointed suspiciously to a diagnosis of dry rot.

The cabin looked well lived in, with jeans, dirty sweats, underwear, towels, books, and other assorted gear sprinkled around the cushioned benches. There was a stack of unwashed dishes in the sink and several empty beer cans on the center table. A fly buzzed around an open jar of peanut butter on the drain.

The counter extended for several feet along the port bulkhead, holding a neat collection of specimen bottles, mostly filled with dirty water and an assortment of seaweed, and pieces of equipment one might expect to find in a marine studies lab. Not elaborate, but giving every indication this operation was what Preston said it was. Forward, the storage bulkheads offered more evidence of student involvement, with hand calculators, swim trunks, scuba gear, more books, and backpacks. Nothing out of the ordinary here.

Scott was halfway up the gangway when he heard Erin's whistle. He grabbed the top rail, took the rest of the ladder up in one swing. He stepped out onto the deck to the distant putter of a small outboard. He flew across the deck, dropped into the Whaler. Erin undid the lines, and, without exchanging a word, they hand-guided the Whaler along the gunwales of the schooner. Scott pointed to the shore, where the branches of elms and alder brushed the water's surface. They shoved off the *Pilgrim*'s sternpost. The Whaler coasted the twenty or so feet to shore, and they fell under the cover of the trees just as the skiff appeared from the bed to the north with the returning students. There were three boys and two girls, and they were talking and laughing and, fortunately, showing little interest in anything around them.

Should he pull alongside, ask his questions,, and then beat it out of there before the weather turned and the students grew overly curious? There was one problem with that. Five students, by Preston's own admission inexperienced in sail, were not by themselves enough to handle the massive gaff-rigged gear on the *Pilgrim*. Somewhere, there had to be a captain and crew. Scott's hand hesitated on the starter.

It began as a distant buzz. Scott tensed up automatically. "Listen."

Erin was already looking up. The buzz turned into an ear-shattering roar. A float plane dropped from the rise of land to the north. The long wings almost brushed the tops of the trees in its swift descent. The pontoons touched the water, skied down the arm, and coasted to a stop alongside the *Pilgrim*. There was no reason for him to feel this uneasiness. No sense to the cramping in his gut. He'd seen nothing suspicious on the ship, nothing to tie it to the murders. The cabin door opened, and they stepped down onto the pontoon, one tall and blade-thin, Jerry, the other built like a small gorilla, Charlie, their pilot, who could have been the helmsman on the *Pilgrim* for all Scott knew. It was one of those improbabilities, the worst fears come true.

Erin gasped. "Scott, it's those two from the Whaler!"

There was no question. These were the same men who'd shot at him and Dandy on the beach, chased him and Erin in Griffin Bay, the same two who'd struck the man on the deck of the *Pilgrim* that night and thrown him into a watery grave. What an inopportune way to prove he'd been right. He and Erin were alone with two killers in the middle of nowhere, barely hidden by the lacy arms of the trees, a good five hundred yards' distance from the safety of open seas and no way out except the way they came in, past the big ship and the three men.

Scott started to sweat. If they left now they would most certainly be seen. There was, of course, the very real prospect they'd already been spotted from the air. Their one chance, it seemed to Scott, was to get out quickly before the men had time to think.

Scott pressed the starter and nosed the Whaler out of the trees. *Easy. Act normal. They don't know who we are. Not yet!* Erin gripped the cockpit rail so tight her knuckles blanched white. She didn't say a word. They started around the *Pilgrim* by the stern. He didn't need to tell her to keep out of sight. She was as aware as he that if the man recognized them, they would strike swiftly.

Scott eased by the *Pilgrim's* blind side. Perhaps they wouldn't notice. Maybe Charlie and Jerry would think it normal for a runabout to wander into an anchorage miles from nowhere and hide behind the trees. Perhaps they wouldn't be alarmed by the presence of strangers in their hideaway, wouldn't expect them to speak or at least show their faces.

They made it to the opening, and Erin pronounced the bad news. "They're getting back into the plane."

"Hang on!" Scott shoved the stick fully forward. The Whaler's bow shot up like a bird in flight, and they vaulted out into the open bay. "We'll hit for Government dock." It was his second mistake.

The plane's engine did another job on their ears as it poised for takeoff.

"Maybe they're just flying out again."

It was a good thought. The plane didn't take off at all. By running, Scott had only confirmed to himself the paranoid fears of the two. The plane cruised behind the Whaler. Capable of speeds upward of sixty-five knots, Scott guessed, it was a virtual certainty the plane could overtake the Whaler, whose maximum speed was closer to forty. The clouds to the north extended, and ahead the water stirred restlessly. He couldn't keep the Whaler at even these speeds in choppy seas. The plane, with her big pontoons, on the other hand, would have much less trouble handling the chop, and if the ride grew too bumpy, could always lift off and fly above it.

Scott abandoned the straight course and took a southwest heading. They would have a better chance, he reasoned, if they hugged the shore. Wings, after all, weren't made to navigate through tree branches. The plane was faster, but the Whaler more maneuverable.

"There are rocks in here," Erin warned.

"We've not much more than a foot of draught, and the tide's up. We should manage it." He didn't want to tell her that, rocks or no, they had no choice.

Behind them, great gushers of water spurted up from under the plane's pontoons, bearing in on them fast. Scott began a zigzagging course across the channel. The pilot made an adjustment and followed.

"He's going to head us off."

Certainly he had the speed for it. Scott took a starboard turn and circled back toward the east shore. Across the small fetch of water, the plane corrected, slowed, and stopped. Scott turned on the wheel and circled again, but the plane, with its wide spread of wings, blocked the entrance to the bay. "He's waiting for us."

A soft breeze put little wavelets over the water. It was still clear sky to the southwest, but the clouds had extended overhead. The wind couldn't have come at a worse time. Right now they needed speed, and they weren't likely to get it if the seas turned to chop. Maybe, he thought hopefully, we can outrun the weather, pass up Evans Bay, and head straight for Quadra, hope the fuel holds out. But getting into open waters remained a problem, since the plane sat squarely in their path.

Providence offered a helping hand. Erin observed it first. The plane was dead in the water. On the pontoon, the pilot had the engine cowling off. Engine trouble. There would never be a better chance. Scott opened her up. The Whaler hurtled forward, picked up speed, scalded past the silver wings, close enough to read her numbers, close enough, he feared, for Charlie and Jerry to confirm what they must already have guessed, close enough to feel their rage, to sense the frustration. Scott saw it first as a flash of light from the cabin door—an arm lifted, taking aim. The report from the gun resounded like a thunderclap across the narrow bay.

"They're shooting at us!"

"Get down on the floor!"

Erin dropped to her knees as bullets spit into the wind around them. One struck the cockpit windshield and shattered the glass.

"Scott!"

"I'm all right. Stay down!" His knees felt like jelly as he held tight to the wheel. Boulders and swift currents marked the passages here, but he knew his chances of maneuvering the tricky passageways was better than escaping a bullet from determined killers. He twisted back and forth crazily. More blasts sounded behind them, but the marksmanship of the gunman, impaired by the bounce of the boat, was fortunately poor. Only a few more minutes and they would be out of range; only a few more zigging turns and they would reach the protection of Bird Cove. Only a few more pounding seconds and his heart would start beating normally again.

The bends in the shore would put them out of range, or so Scott hoped. He zipped into the trees at full speed. Rock outcroppings rose dangerously from the shoreline, but Scott gave no thought to the prop or the boat's fiberglass bottom, for here, he felt certain, the plane couldn't follow, and he much preferred a torn-up hull or a bent prop to a hole in his head.

Erin came up off the floor to brave a look. "I don't see them. Maybe they've given up."

He wished he could believe it. For the moment they were out of firing range, but the pilot could get their plane in the air again at any time. With this in mind, Scott cut along the beach, continuing to dodge the rocks and limbs of trees. Still no sign of the plane. It was time to take another chance.

"Where now?" Erin asked.

"We head for home."

"Do you think they'll follow?"

He imagined they would try. Across the open waters between Read and Quadra, a seagull hovered suspended in the air by the force of freshening winds, and he had new concerns. The waves were piling up with surprising strength, and the gray look that had threatened to the north had spread over the south as well. Added to this, the gas gauge, which had been gyrating undependably around the quarter-full mark, now pointed to empty. He had the five gallons in reserve, but was it enough to take them to Rebecca Spit? One thing he was learning about the Mercury: that big engine had an insatiable thirst. They were a mile out in open seas when it produced the first telltale sputters. Erin's face read alarm.

"We're out of gas."

"I'll switch over to the reserve tank."

He flicked off the engine and repositioned the spare tank.

He had time to think as they rolled around in the chop, engine dead, while he attached the hose to the reserve tank and hand-primed gas into the new line. Why had those two returned to the *Pilgrim*? Was the *Pilgrim* a cover, and, if so, what did this say about Preston Fields?

Scott tried the engine. The *Mercury* coughed. He tried again. It sputtered and shook. Nothing. He returned to the engine well, went through it all another time, squeezed the hose, tried to feed fuel through. The waves threw them around, and Erin looked a little sick. "I'll try now. Should work."

He turned on the starter. The *Mercury* sputtered, stopped; they continued to bounce. He turned it on a second time. It choked, gasped, stuttered into a rumble, and they started out once more, Erin looking sickly pale but much relieved.

Their best hope of making it on the reserve was to head straight for Quadra. The problem was weather. The waves were turning wild, forcing him to cut his speed. With the wind also came cold. In her light jacket, Erin shivered. "Let's button her up. At least we can keep the wind out."

Erin worked quietly beside him, snapping the plastic covers into place. Zipped up, the plastic shut out the wind, as he'd said, but they quickly saw a new problem. The plastic reduced their visibility so severely that Scott couldn't judge the water's twists and turns, slowing them all the more.

"Better to see," Erin decided.

They knocked down again. The changeovers took time, and each howl of the wind brought renewed fears the plane would return. Someone had once said boating was a continual trade-off. The Whaler, for example, was the right boat for calm seas, and got places in a hurry. Coming up in the Whaler, they'd made good time. Now, in the cresting waves, they could only inch along; the shoreline passed so slowly, at times it appeared they were standing still. For these seas, a sailboat was what he needed. As the weather worsened, Scott wished fervently he had the *Picaroon* under his feet.

"I think I see the Spit."

He saw nothing but another rise of land. He didn't want to tell Erin, but by his calculations they were a good ten miles from the marina. What ran through his mind now were alternatives. He could take a heading to Read's west side so that if the storm raged out of control, he could run the Whaler up on the beach. There were problems with that, too. If he spent too much time off his heading they could run out of gas. This he feared most at this point. Hard to spot a small boat tossing helplessly in whirling seas. Should he go for the beach or try for Rebecca Spit?

"I'm sure I see it," Erin shouted.

He saw, too. A ten-minute run. At these speeds, twenty? Hug the shore or cut into the open and fight the cross chop? Forget the plane. Erin had her eyes on the water directly ahead.

"Rock!"

A large boulder burst out of the trough, just off their bow. Scott held his breath and spun the wheel, caught a roll. More rocks erupted off their side. He spun again. The Whaler nosed up out of the water, lifted above the swirling waves, spinning dizzily, and fell back, bow down, stern up. The engine faltered, and Erin groaned. Scott let go the wheel. The Whaler dropped back, reeling into the swell. They bounced over another wave, ballast gone, the engine doing a good imitation of a dying drum. His neck and shoulders ached from straining to see. Erin's eyes riveted on the auxiliary tank.

"We're out of gas," she said.

"No." Not yet, they weren't. "She stalled when we came out of the water."

Scott had been so busy at the wheel that he hadn't heard the sound of the giant engine or seen the pontoons settling over them like a dark rain cloud ready to burst. There was no time to worry about their dwindling supply of fuel or the forces of the wind. Ahead was Rebecca Spit, where there were people and telephones. Hovering over them was the float plane carrying the two men who had killed at least one person, possibly three. And he and Erin were the only ones around to tell.

Off their port, a roller threw its spume thirty feet into the air, and overhead silver wings dipped and lifted, the rumble of the plane's giant engine muffled by the wind. Scott cranked the wheel into the chop. Only a few yards now, the long sandy strip of land rose in front of them. The plane banked. Scott slid toward the dock, and the plane carrying Charlie and Jerry turned and headed north.

Twenty

Out of gas and floundering, the Whaler caught a rush of wind, blew against the dock, and thumped into the hands of a stranger. "I've got her!" It was a deep, wheezing voice. A giant of a man stood on the float and held off the bow, preventing another collision with the dock.

Scott and Erin jumped onto the float beside him, and the three tied the boat to the cleats so she still bobbed restlessly in the chop, but without scraping.

"There, that's a proper job," the big man wheezed. His name was George Storey, and he was the owner of the marina. He had thick reddish-gray hair and a full beard, stood between six and seven feet, and to Scott was as welcome as Santa Claus to a child at Christmas. "Rough going," the big man said, tossing his head at the big breakers slamming against the floats.

Scott nodded, and then, because it was uppermost in his mind, said, "Is there a phone we could use?"

"Just up the hill."

Besides running the gas dock and the moorage, Storey and his wife rented rooms from their home that sat high above the marina overlooking the strait. "Americans, are you?" he said as he led Erin and Scott up a steep path to the house, pausing often to get his breath and running words together when he talked. "We're used to the squalls. They always take strangers by surprise."

"Do they last long?" Erin asked.

"Not unless it's the beginning of a weather change. Can hang on for days. Even the ferry shuts down when the gales come up."

Erin took this news with a look of total rejection, which didn't go unnoticed by the big man. "Don't worry," he said with a bearded grin. "Looks like this one will blow out by morning." He stopped at a small rise to catch his breath. "There's a silver lining to this," he wheezed. "My wife's a very good cook."

Erin smiled, but Scott knew she was thinking about Al and that they were already overdue in Campbell River.

The Storey house was a modified Cape Cod, shingle-sided and weathered a pale gray, which tended to confirm what Storey said about the storms that struck this corner of the island on a regular basis. The Storeys were a congenial couple who had mastered the act of making their guests feel at home. Martha Storey was a dimply, cheerful, middle-aged woman with a plump figure and snappy dark eyes, and from the aromas that floated out of her kitchen, all her husband promised in the culinary department. She also enjoyed fussing over people, which her husband attributed to the fact that she'd looked after four daughters, all married and gone now, and couldn't get out of the habit.

"Poor things," she said, taking one look at Scott and Erin. "Never mind, a wash-up and a hot cup of tea will set you right."

Scott placed his first call to the RCMP in Campbell River. The officer took it all down: the description of the plane, the numbers, which Scott remembered after some mind-jogging from Erin, the location of the *Pilgrim*, and Leroy's private line in Friday Harbor. The officer wasn't particularly optimistic about finding Charlie and Jerry. A small plane could fly across borders faster than customs could track them, he said, and it was his guess these two would get as far from Campbell River as possible. He promised to do his best.

Erin accepted the judgment of the RCMP happily. "That means they won't be back."

"They're out to save their own skins now," Scott agreed.

Scott called next to alert Leroy, but reached Harold instead, who promised to deliver the message. Erin placed a call to Al. Professor Turner was out, the hotel operator told her. Erin left a message, and Scott promised they'd try again later. Thoroughly cheered, they put themselves in Martha Storey's hands.

158

She served them hot tea and biscuits fresh out of the oven, a delicious little raisin cake that dripped with melted butter, fresh strawberry jam—homemade—and a small glob of whipped cream. Scott put three away without a trace of conscience while they got acquainted with the Storeys.

Outside, the sky continued to darken, and Erin grew anxious about Al. "Isn't there a chance we can get back today?"

George walked over to the barometer that hung beside the kitchen clock, studied it a moment, and returned shaking his head. "You won't want to take that little boat around the Cape today. Only last month a big trawler went down in winds just like this."

"We have two lovely rooms," Martha said. "You can stay the night and get a fresh start in the morning."

Al must have been waiting by the phone. Erin barely got a word in. Scott could hear him from across the room. "Rebecca Spit? Where the devil is that? I expected you back an hour ago."

Erin took some time trying to placate him, and Scott finally took over. "Sorry, Al, we ran into some weather."

The old man sniffed irritably. "I can see that. I told you, didn't I?"

"You did, and you were right."

When Scott finished explaining about the risks of running in the storm, Al's voice softened. "Stay put till it clears."

As George had predicted, the weather worsened. With the wind still wailing outside, they dined with the Storeys. After dinner, Erin and Martha sat on the big plumped-up living-room sofa and exchanged recipes and decorating ideas, a conversation that drew an amused smile from George, who rested his big frame in a leather reclining chair. Scott stood by the window watching the giant rollers breaking over the rocks, wondering if it would quit by morning. In the fireplace, wood cracked and spit as the wind sucked the flames up the stack.

"Martha tells me you're a surgeon," George said. Erin had let that information out of the bag.

"Yes," Scott said.

"Tired of it, are you?"

"Does it show that much?"

"Most people vacation to get a break from what they do. They're usually busting to go back after a week or two, especially industrious fellows like yourself."

"Don't you ever tire of what you do?"

"Haven't been at it that long. I was a floor man—knees gave out, and lungs. The doc said clean air, and we came here. That was seven years ago."

"And you still like it?"

"Once in a while you get unpleasant guests, and you think about chucking it. But most people are nice, and it's good fun."

The rooming arrangements were puritan. Scott's room was down and across the hall from Erin. At her door, Scott looked into her sleepy face, so pale in the shadowed hall, and felt guilty. "Sorry about the day."

"Why?" she said, stopping a yawn.

"Getting you into another mess."

"It was a wonderful day," she said, smiling.

As George had promised, the morning restored summer to the Spit. The water was like a duck pond, and the heat of the sun sent a layer of steam off the docks. They filled the Whaler's gas tanks, Scott paid the modest bill for the lodging, and they parted with the Storeys with much laughing and promises to return.

Waiting at the marina in Campbell River, Al looked happy to see them. Scott arbitrated with the manager of the marina over the damages to the windshield and the extra day, finally settling on a price slightly greater than Scott thought it worth, and they left, everyone talking at once.

"How did you get that hole in the glass?" Al asked suspiciously as they walked across the Quay.

Erin told Al about the chase, never quite getting around to the shooting, which only aroused the old man's suspicions the more. She soft-pedaled it about the plane having engine trouble and what the police had said, but Al saw through it and didn't like it. "Scottie, from here on out, let Leroy handle it!"

160

It was quickly apparent on the drive back to Sidney that Al had learned something from his library prowlings but was going to pick his own good time to tell it. Erin knew the signs, too: the silent smile; the slow stoking of his pipe; the meaningless chatter about the weather, the scenery, and the cost of the rooms, which he thought exorbitant. It was all designed to drive them crazy, and Erin endured it for most of an hour before she said, "Come on, Grandpa, let's hear it."

"I was in the library most of the day yesterday." He chuckled. "You wouldn't believe it, Scottie. Wonderful collection. First editions, antiquities, modern material, all well researched, nicely collated."

Erin started to laugh. "C'mon, Grandpa, you've had your fun. Tell us. You know you're dying to."

"I did pick up one bit of information I thought curious. Don't know that it matters now that we're turning this all over to Leroy, but I asked about the history of Canadian industry. Recent history, of course. They had some fascinating pamphlets about people who had their start in Campbell River and went on to achieve fame and fortune, like the well-known educator and conservationist Roderick Haig-Brown."

"I remember that name," Erin said. "We saw some of his books in Victoria."

"Yes, you would. He was a chancellor of the University of Victoria. Anyway, he comes from Campbell River. And guess who else comes from these parts? Brice Randall."

It was like hearing a voice from a dream. Butterflies started floating around Scott's stomach. Erin looked a little sick.

"Grandpa, what are you trying to say?"

"Not trying to say anything, except isn't it a great big coincidence that the big-shot developer from Seattle got his start in land development in Campbell River?"

Twenty-One

In the morning a light rain pitted the gentle waters of Cattle Pass and put a chill on the summer air. A front coming off the Pacific would continue to bring unstable weather to the region, the forecasters said. Scott made his call to Perth, Australia.

"No," his party concluded after five minutes of questions and intermittent pauses, "I don't know anything about it." The voice on the other end was definite and aroused, and later, Scott knew, there'd be more questions, accusations. Scott didn't relish causing trouble, even for someone he'd never liked, but there came a point when there was no choice, and he'd already passed it.

His first stop was only a few hundred yards down the road where the big house on the point was immersed in the heavy cloud layer that had settled over the Cape. Henry Mason, bundled up in an old army surplus jacket, was exercising the black Labs in the woods behind the house. The murders had intensified his basically untrusting nature. "What about Brice Randall?" he said, considering Scott suspiciously across the kennel yard.

"Is he solvent?"

"He has an A-1 credit rating from Dun and Bradstreet," Henry said, amused by the question. "And he has friends at City Hall. Cuts his risk, if you see what I mean." Randall had done very well, Henry said. Had only one flaw. "He likes the ladies."

This wasn't at all the kind of information Scott wanted to hear.

From Henry's, Scott drove directly to the sheriff's office. Harold looked up from Leroy's desk and cheerfully delivered his news. They'd identified the man hauled up in the fishermen's nets as a treasury agent. On this news, Scott dropped into a chair.

"Yeah, Leroy flew to Seattle an hour ago to meet with the federal boys. It's their case now. Too bad you missed all the fun, Doc. We ran all over your beach yesterday, looking for that .38. Found it, too. And guess what. The FBI came up with a positive ID on those two who broke into your place. One of them is wanted for killing a bank clerk in Boston."

Scott felt a sick pitch in his stomach, remembering how close he and Erin had come to being one of his victims. "Does Leroy think they're the ones who murdered Owen and Marilyn?"

"Not much doubt of it."

Scott's pulse raced as he left Harold and headed for the university experimental lab. He found Preston Fields slumped over his desk, the picture of dejection. In the few days since their last meeting, his boyish look had disappeared. Preston had aged ten years. "The *Pilgrim?*" he repeated dully, looking back at Scott through the heavy-rimmed glasses. "I don't understand."

"Cut the games, Pres. You're covering for men who killed a treasury agent, and I talked to the dean. The university did not authorize the use of the *Pilgrim* for research. You did!"

Preston jerked back as though he'd been struck. "You called Corny? In Australia?" His face twitched in anger. "For your information, I just talked to my students. They're in Campbell River, flying back here this afternoon, and, for the record, it wasn't my idea."

"Whose, then?"

"I'm not at liberty to say."

Scott stared at him in disbelief. "With four people dead?"

A dark flush rose from under Preston's collar. "What do you mean four?"

"Had you forgotten Toni?" It was, of course, only a hunch.

The muscles around Preston's mouth twitched again. "That was an accident. Wasn't it?"

Scott shook his head. "C'mon, Pres, give!"

Preston sighed unhappily and finally began to tell his story. It all started in the spring, he said, when some of the people in town complained that students from his lab were pushing narcotics on the local kids. Preston looked into it and found a few pot smokers, but no evidence of hard drugs.

Not long after, a man walked into his office who said he was a treasury agent, gave his name as Don Smith. He was working undercover on a drug ring operating in the islands and said university students might be involved. He said they'd discovered drugs in the storage barrels used by the lab on their research ships and suspected students or staff of bringing it in from Central America.

"I imagine you were pretty upset."

Preston looked up through angry eyes. "I was pissed! To think of anyone jeopardizing this important work—for profit, for drug running."

"What did you do?"

"What could I do? I appealed to Smith, told him about our grants and what we're trying to do here. He said he only wanted the ones who'd engineered the whole business, that he'd keep us out of the news if I'd cooperate."

"And you agreed?"

"Didn't think I had a choice. Anyway, a few weeks before that I'd received a letter from an outfit called Camstar, who said they owned this schooner and were looking for a tax write-off. They'd studied our program and were particularly impressed by our work on the moon snails. They offered the use of the *Pilgrim* and a crew. I don't know how, but Smith knew all about that offer. I was going to reject it. With all the liability problems, it sounded hare-brained to me. That's when Smith showed up and asked me to accept and put him on board as a visiting professor, which I did."

"Did Smith communicate with you during the time he was on the ship?"

"After about a week, he called, said he was making progress.

He didn't believe any of the students on the *Pilgrim* were involved, but there could be involvement from here."

"Did he call again?"

Preston nodded glumly. "He stopped in about two weeks ago, said he was getting close, that he expected a big shipment, and I got the idea that would be the end of it."

"When?"

"Before the end of the month, I think." He shook his head. "Don't hold me to it."

"In the name of heaven, weren't you even curious?"

"No!" Preston grew defiant. "And I'll tell you something else. I wish I'd never allowed myself to be talked into it in the first place. What good has it done me? I allowed our students to go out with known felons. I didn't know, but do you think the dean will believe that? And no one's proved to me any of our people were in on it, anyway."

"Okay, Pres, Smith said the end of the month. This is the twenty-eighth. When is the big research ship due back from Panama?"

"Sometime today."

"And you told no one about Smith?"

Preston shook his head wearily. "I only learned about his death this morning. Heard it on the news. I've been sitting here ever since, wondering what in hell to do."

"Call Leroy. What else?"

With a defeated droop to his shoulders, Preston nodded. They'd never been friends, but at this moment, watching Preston's neat, orderly world split apart, Scott couldn't help feeling sorry for him.

"About Toni, Scott. I only know what I read in the papers, that it was an accident or a suicide."

Strangely, this time Scott felt no pain at the words. "Neither one. She had enough Valium in her system to put down a horse. She was allergic to Valium. She would never have taken it voluntarily."

"Sorry," Preston said softly. "So sorry. But why did you think

I would know anything about it? There was never anything between Toni and me."

Getting an uneasy sensation in the pit of his stomach, Scott walked to the window and looked across the harbor at the boats swinging in the wind. "You were seen with her at Owen's parties."

"I saw her at Owen's once or twice, but she never came with me. Why don't you ask the man who brought her?"

Scott felt a tingling in his neck that started down his spine. He turned and searched Preston's bewildered face. "Who?" he asked, steeling himself for the answer. "Who should I ask?"

"But I thought you knew. Fred! Why don't you ask Fred?"

It was a long drive back to the Cape in the rain. Water flooded the windshield, and through the glass the whole world was a thick gray mist. Toni and Fred! It had been there in front of him all the time. Fred, charming, affable, attractive, a man who seldom had a serious thought, and Toni, who loved a good time. The wind kicked up off the strait and blew the rain harder against the glass, totally blotting out the trees and the road. Dandy stirred restlessly beside him, and Scott reduced his speed to a crawl.

His wife and his best friend, the two couples, both childless, always together, the knowing glances, all overlooked. So many little things now clear. Lorene and her trip abroad. What was it Cynthia had said, that Lorene had gone off the deep end for a while? Fred so distraught when he brought the news of Toni's death. Scott shook his head to dislodge the suspicions and stared bleakly at the rain-pelted road.

A squall ripped up the waters of Cattle Pass as Scott turned into his drive. Dandy raced for the door. Scott trudged dispiritedly behind. "We'll get a fire going," he said, shivering. But he knew it wasn't the rain or the sharp wind blowing off the strait that chilled him down to his toes.

There was something. Owen? What was Fred doing at Owen's parties? He'd always professed to detest Owen and his soirees. And Toni's picture in Owen's wallet. No sense to it. Had

Lorene known? The presumption was she had. Scott shook his head sadly, thinking of the pain it had brought to them all. A blast of wind threw a sheet of spray against the big living-room windows. Water rolled down the outer glass and dripped off the sill onto the deck. The memories came in painful flashes, not productive, best forgotten. Scott gave up plans to go by Fish Creek and talk to Vic. The questions he'd wanted to ask his friend seemed suddenly unimportant. Even the murders were blotted out by the pain of knowing he'd lived for months or years with a delusion about his wife and his best friend.

"Forget Toni," Ralph had said, "she's not right for you, never was." Could it be his partner had known, too? Maybe everyone had known but him.

The phone's ring jarred like an unwanted visitor. It was Leroy, returned from Seattle. "Where you been, Doc? Been trying to reach you for two days." Before Scott could answer, he said, "Guess I have you to thank for that half-witted professor finally coming forward. Can you believe a well-educated man could be so stupid?"

Scott only half listened while Leroy told him about Preston and the *Pilgrim* and the drug ring. The treasury people would make an arrest within hours, Leroy said.

"Mmm," Scott said, unable to get excited at the news.

"Say, is something wrong with you? You sound all washed out."

"No," Scott lied. "Tired, that's all." He wished Leroy well, and when he put the phone down remembered he hadn't asked who was behind the whole operation. Then, as he started sorting it out, he began the painful process of answering his own question.

He couldn't accept the idea that Charlie and Jerry had gone on an aimless killing spree. There had to be a reason for each killing. Easy to understand the treasury agent. Smith had found them out, and they'd struck him senseless, thrown him overboard to protect their own skins. But why Owen? He was a key man in the drug scheme, on the same side. And why Marilyn? She'd talked out of turn, but how could they have known, unless someone told them? Who? Bob? If his grief over his wife's death wasn't real, he was a hell of an actor. Who else knew of Marilyn's rantings? Almost everyone at the party, as well as Vic, Georgie, and the fishermen.

Another question that had bothered him from the start. Why break into Scott's house, tear everything upside down, and take nothing? He sat with that a minute; then it stirred, a notion buried deep. He dug it out of the bedroom bureau drawer— Toni's evening bag. This time he searched its insides. Comb, lip gloss, wallet, key, everything except the one item Charlie and Jerry had broken into his house to find. Toni's appointment book was gone, and there was only one other person who'd known of its existence.

Scott shook his head, in rejection or denial he wasn't sure which. He was, he decided, looking at it from the wrong side, needed a clinical view. Read the symptoms before making the diagnosis. He thought about obsessions, about a look in an unguarded moment, about emotional imbalance, and about the unstable mind driven too far. Sadly, it began to make sense. With dread, Scott made the calls to Seattle, asked the questions that only confirmed what he'd begun to suspect. He shoved a log on the fire and watched unhappily as it exploded up the stack.

He was considering the alarming drift of his findings and wondering what he should do when Dandy alerted him to a visitor at their front door. It was Al. He was wearing the old yellow rain slicker with the big floppy hat, and the water spilled off the brim like the runoff from an overfull gutter as he stood in the darkened doorway.

"Come on in, Al. Get that wet stuff off and pull up a seat by the fire."

Al shook his head and didn't budge, and Scott saw he was upset. "Where's Erin?"

"I hoped she was here."

"No. Has she been gone?"

"Couple hours. Left after dinner."

She'd probably got hung up in town. Scott pulled the old boy over the threshold and shut the door on a rush of wind. "If she drove into town, she'll be a while. Hard to see a thing on that road in this weather, believe me. I crawled back myself. Don't worry. She's a good driver. She'll be along soon."

"She didn't go to town."

Scott got an uneasy feeling. "Where did she go?"

"It was all that stuff about Brice Randall." He shook his head in disgust, and water from the rain jacket splashed onto the floor. "Sorry. I told you I was wet."

"Never mind that. Where the hell *did* she go?"

"She said she was going to check on Owen's artifacts."

"You mean she went to Owen's?" Scott's voice lifted. "You let her go alone to Owen's?"

"I didn't let her do a darned thing," Al said morosely. "She called Millie to see if Millie could let her in, so she could take a quick look. Satisfy herself, she said."

"So she met Millie at Owen's?" Scott sighed with inner relief. "Come on, we'll go over and roust her. Millie's quite a talker when she gets started."

Al shook his head. "She didn't meet Millie. That's what I've been trying to tell you. Millie was busy, suggested Erin ask one of the neighbors to let her in. You know how everyone around this Cape has a key to his neighbor's in case of fire when they're off the island?"

"So who had a key to Owen's?" Scott asked, feeling a tightening in his chest.

"Fred and Lorene. Erin said she was going to stop by their place, but that was two hours ago. I called Fred; got no answer. Called Owen's, and the phone's been disconnected. Guess I should walk over there." Al stopped talking and looked at Scott. "Something's wrong."

Scott was already at the phone dialing the familiar numbers. He let it ring a dozen times before he finally replaced the receiver and looked into Al's anxious face. "Al," he said, working to keep the fear out of his voice, "Erin's probably gone over to Owen's with

Fred, and Fred's as big a gossip as Millie. Why don't you take Dandy, run along home, and fix a drink. I'll fetch Erin and join you in a few minutes."

Relief poured into the old man's face.

Scott waited only until Al and Dandy were out the door and then rushed back to the phone, placed the hurried call to Leroy, told him what he knew—or thought he knew—finished in a rush of words, and rang off, leaving the sheriff to fill in the rest. Leroy could handle the drug shipment. More important to Scott was Erin. He'd failed Toni. He wouldn't fail Erin.

Twenty-Two

The Jeep lurched as the heavy truck wheels struck the potholes on Beach Lane. Erin is all right, Scott told himself over and over. She won't be harmed, not if she doesn't say anything about the *Pilgrim* or the land deals in Campbell River, and there's no reason she would. The masks! Would she feel she had to explain about Owen's artifacts? Would she tell what she'd undoubtedly guessed, that they were all fakes, substituted for the ones Randall had purchased from Owen for cash?

A normal person wouldn't kill for so little. But this wasn't a normal person. This was a deranged and highly dangerous paranoid schizophrenic who'd already killed twice and wouldn't hesitate to kill again. Such a person would quickly assume Erin knew it all—the elaborate scheme for laundering drug money, the network of pleasure and fishing boats, of university ships used to smuggle drugs into the islands, and the identity of the one who'd put it all together, the unlikely person with the cunning and the obsessed determination of the mad.

Scott jammed his foot on the accelerator, and the Jeep bounced onto the Cape road. If only he'd taken the trouble to pursue the thing with Randall. If only he'd wrung the truth out of Preston long ago. If only he'd known about Fred and Toni, recognized those early signs of something wrong, he might have prevented four murders. And Erin—it was like the night they found Toni, the nightmare all over again.

Owen's roof rose out of the rain-soaked scrub trees. Scott took the turn into the drive on two wheels and braked the Jeep.

He ran to the door, saw that it was ajar, and burst in, calling Erin's name. Silence greeted him. As on the morning they found Owen, even the wind's howl had no chance against the double-paned glass that insulated the rooms.

The room looked much as it had the morning they'd found Owen lying in the pool of his own blood, except the ugly patch of red no longer stained the living-room carpet, and the trays of cigarette ashes and clam dips were gone. The place was immaculate, undoubtedly from Millie's earnest efforts. Even the sofa was restored to a milk white, and the curved sections returned to their places around the spot where Owen had fallen. The smell of death, shut in by the thick doors and windows, a house closed up in the summer heat, remained. Scott stared painfully at the walls. The gaping ebony faces, the long-jawed pieces of petrified wood that held the grim secrets of the life-and-death struggle that had taken place here, laughed back.

Scott started through the rooms, fearful of what he might find, more fearful of not knowing. Kitchen—empty. Halls—still. Utility—washer, dryer, closets—all empty. Bedrooms—spotless. Then he saw it on the dressing-room floor, shockingly brilliant against the white marble floor tiles, the small cloth of silk with the geometric swirls of bright blues and reds. Scott picked it up, held it in his hand, and breathed in the scent of Erin's perfume—the scarf he'd bought for her that day in Victoria. "I'm a summer, didn't you know?" she had said with the teasing laugh. "But I love bright colors." Scott's spirits soared as he clutched the certain evidence Erin had been here, and, just as swiftly, sank. She'd been here, all right, but clearly she was gone now, and her fate was more uncertain than before. There was only one other place to look.

He ran out the door and sprinted over the sandy hump, stumbled in the dark through the grove of Scotch pine, and splashed across the water-soaked dirt path. Out of breath and thoroughly drenched, he landed at Fred's back porch. The door was unlocked. He rushed in, took two sloshing steps into the kitchen, and stared into the surprised face of his best friend. "Fred, what the hell you doing here?"

172

Recovering, Fred said, "I live here, remember?" Then, "My God, Scottie, you're raining all over the floor."

Scott still wasn't absolutely sure, still didn't want to believe. "Don't you ever answer your phone?"

Fred laughed. "Oh, that. Sorry, Scottie. I thought it was the office. Meant to take the phone off the hook."

Typical, Fred's way of not facing things.

"What's up, ol' buddy? You don't look too happy."

"Where's Lorene and Erin?"

"They went out for a while. Anything wrong?"

"Where did they go?"

"Umm. I think they said they were stopping at Owen's. Something about the masks."

"They're not there."

"Umm. Probably went to town. Lorene said something earlier about needing a few things at the store." Fred's eyes flickered. "There *is* something wrong. What is it?"

Scott shook his head. All seemingly normal. Was it possible Fred didn't know? He looked into the open, friendly face and wondered why he'd never guessed about Toni. Nothing could stay hidden on that face. It was simply that he hadn't been looking. Suddenly, without good reason, Scott felt a surge of sympathy for his friend, and then new fear.

"Fred, does Lorene ever take the Bayliner out by herself?"

"All the time. Didn't you know? She handles the thing better than I do. 'Course, she's a bit reckless. Goes out at the oddest times." He sighed deeply. "I suppose she feels the need to get away." He shook his head, and an inexplicable sadness came over his face. Scott thought how truly blind he'd been to his friend's needs. "Why do I get a feeling you're trying to tell me something?"

"I'm worried about Erin, Fred. Do you think they might have gone out in the boat?"

Fred glanced out the window at the rollers crashing against the rocks below his deck. "In this stuff? My God, I hope not."

"I think I'll just swing by the creek," Scott said.

Fred got a look in his eyes. He pulled his jacket off the hall peg and started behind Scott. "I think I'll go with you."

Vic and Georgie popped out of the doghouse when Scott and Fred reached the creek. "Yeah, I saw them." Vic shoved an arm into the sleeves of his rain slicker. "Thought it damn weird, going for a joyride in this slop."

"Which way they headed?"

"South, I think." Vic studied Scott's face. "Something wrong, huh?"

"I have to catch them, Vic."

Beside Scott, Fred dripped rain and grew anxious. "What the hell is this all about, Scottie?"

"I'm not sure. You better stay here."

"The hell I will. What's going on? Let's have it."

Scott took a deep breath and through the blinding rain faced the dark, worried eyes. "I think Lorene's involved in a drug-smuggling operation." Scott stopped, couldn't tell him the rest.

Fred's mouth gaped. A lightning bolt couldn't have jolted him more. "You can't be serious."

"Wish I weren't." There was no time—no time to go into it now.

Vic had the picture. "Davey's bow picker is the fastest thing around."

There were few surprises among the fishermen, who all along had known more about the whole business than they'd let on, about Lorene and her night runs, about the lights off Iceberg. While Fred watched, angry, bewildered, Davey revved up the big diesel.

"About time someone did something," Davey said. "Get aboard."

Scott climbed over the side. Fred leaped after him. "I'm going, and when I prove you wrong, you'll eat shit." The rainwater slid down his cheeks like tears. "I thought you were my friend."

It was like having a knife twisted inside him. Scott wished he was wrong, that he'd read all the signs incorrectly, that Lorene hadn't committed the terrible crimes in order to protect what she thought needed protecting, to save all she cared about in the world—her husband.

Georgie undid the lines on the *Mollie O* and boarded. "You might need an extra hand."

The *Mollie O* was an open boat, a small cabin aft and the spool and the wheel forward, mostly built for speed. From the deck of the *Nellie J*, Vic cupped his hands around his mouth and yelled, "We'll follow. Keep your channels open."

Scott waited by the rail and wished they'd get started.

Davey backed the *Mollie O* out of the slip, and, driving into sheets of rain, headed out. "Where to?"

"Around the lighthouse, out there with the blinking lights."

"Iceberg?"

No, not if he was right. If it were as Scott feared, she'd be going north. "Up Haro."

They shot out of the creek. Fred stared glumly over the rail. He was beginning to get an inkling of what was going on, and growing more fearful by the minute. "You can't think Lorene had anything to do with these murders." His voice pleaded for support.

Scott couldn't bring himself to answer.

"You nuts, Scottie? Lorene wouldn't hurt a fly."

"What about Toni, Fred?"

Fred's face was a mix of horror and guilt. "Toni was an accident." But his voice held less conviction than before.

Davey took the turn out of the creek and caught a roller. The *Mollie O* lurched. The wind howled so loudly Scott had to shout to be heard. "The Lorene we know wouldn't. This is a different Lorene—hasn't been herself in months. Swings of mood. Obsessed . . ."

Spray splashed over the rails. Fred's lips trembled. No words came out.

"Something threatened her, and like a circuit breaker overloaded, she blew. Happens that way sometimes."

"She worries about things," Fred blurted. "Who doesn't?"

"And the trip to Switzerland? I talked to your doctor, Fred. It's more than that, and you know it."

"Fuckin' doctors. All stick together." Fred said something more that Scott missed. Then, "How did you know about Switzerland?"

"Cynthia."

"Don't know what Cynthia told you . . . wasn't anything like that. Lorene had a case of nerves. I'm not the easiest person to live with, you know. She'd been upset, losing her parents. But she's okay now. You're wrong. You'll see." Fred took a blast of wind and sea in the face. He licked the salt off his lips and slumped against the rail, looking miserably unsure.

Scott could find no words to comfort him. All he could think of was Erin alone with madness and nowhere to run.

At the helm, Davey was having his own problems trying to get full speed out of his boat. "Wish I could open her up. Too much chop."

Scott nodded grimly and told himself for the hundredth time that it was not too late. They have a head start, but Lorene won't do anything until she gets well out in the strait and probably not until she meets whoever it is she's racing to meet. On a clear summer day Lorene's Bayliner could outrun most boats. But not tonight, not with the wind gusting and blowing rain in their faces so much that a reef or the unpredictable dips in the waves couldn't be seen. She'd have to slow down, too.

They thumped over a big roller, and Scott hung on to the rail to keep from being swept over the side. He looked quickly for Fred, saw he was clutching the metal sides of the reel, his eyes fixed on the water. Davey's bow picker wasn't as fast as the Bayliner, but it had the durability of a tug and handled better in heavy seas. On this, Scott pinned his hopes.

Around Seal Rock, the waves rolled in from the north, building to six-foot peaks. They went through rocking, putting spray across the decks, but never losing forward momentum. Past the point they ran into a cross chop. The *Mollie O* pitched, but only slightly. It would be a problem for the lighter Bayliner. This prompted a new fear. Scott prayed Lorene was as skilled at handling the small boat as Fred said she was.

Davey took the shortcut between Goose Island and the kelp bed, and drove into the rain and wind coming around the lighthouse. It was like the inside of a mine shaft. The rain fell so hard they couldn't see two feet in front of their bow. But Davey knew every rock and sandbar in the passage. He surged through with his throttle close to wide open. With rain blowing in his eyes, Scott looked for Fred. He saw only a dim outline against the spool.

Vic's voice shouted over the radio. "This is the *Nellie J* calling the *Mollie O*. Come in, *Mollie*."

Davey unhooked the mouthpiece from the radio hanging from his doghouse bulkhead. "This is the *Mollie O*. Go ahead, Vic."

"I'm just rounding the point. Where are you?"

"West of the lighthouse, coming up on the trap. It's black as pitch out here. Can't even see the lights of Victoria."

"Run your floods. Billy's fishing near there. He says he saw the Bayliner shoot past about ten minutes ago with two people aboard."

Scott's spirits lifted. Erin was alive.

"Billie said he isn't doing worth shit with the fishing so he's going to reel in and follow you. You might tell the doc, Billy says he knows all about those blinking lights."

Scott was moved at Billy's sacrifice of a night's fishing.

"Hey," Davey said, "Billy's got two kids. He knows the score."

Fred dropped into a sitting position by the reel and buried his head in his hands. Water ran over his open collar and down his neck. The boat pitched. Fred rolled with it and didn't look up.

Two minutes later they spotted Billy's net. The lights on the gill-netter flickered faintly in the darkness, almost like the lights off Iceberg, signals from those fishing boats involved in an

177

operation more profitable than fishing. Who these fishermen were Scott didn't want to know. He preferred to leave it to Leroy and the treasury men, for he feared there might be among them old friends, men he'd once liked and admired, men who'd worked damn hard for their living; embittered men, recruited by Owen and his cohorts. Scott couldn't condone what they'd done, but he knew the despair that had led them to resort to such desperate acts.

A wave broke over the bow. Its spray illuminated the deck. In the shimmering fountains of water, Scott imagined Erin's blue eyes filled with terror. He pulled his jacket collar tighter around him and shoved his hands in his pockets.

Vic's voice cut in, in a three-way hookup with Billy. "I talked to Leroy. He says there's a big bust going down, somewhere near Davison Head in Speiden Channel."

"Any trouble?" Davey asked.

"Might be. He said we ought to leave it to the professionals."

Billy laughed. "What did you tell him?"

"I told him to blow it out his . . ." The wind and Billy's laughter blotted out the rest.

Davey approached Mitchell Bay and eased up on the throttle. "Do we head outside Henry Island or go through Mosquito?"

There was no way to be sure, but it stood to reason Lorene would take the safer, shorter run through Roche. "Mosquito."

Davey nodded and throttled up, started through the narrow passage between Henry Island and Hanbury Point.

"This gets shoal in here," Scott warned.

There was no need to worry. Davey knew the waterways in the islands as well as Scott knew the veins and arteries through which human life flowed.

Inside the protection of Henry Island the wind died, and in the distance, Scott imagined he heard the sound of another boat. Davey heard, too. He cut his engine, and they bounced through the slop. At first there was only the noise of the water splashing against the sides of the *Mollie O*. Then it broke through, the distant rumble of an engine, falling and rising as it worked through the chop. The lamps from the Roche docks and the lights of a dozen ships bouncing at anchor blinked brightly across the harbor. A veiled specter moved laboriously between them. The Bayliner! Scott's pulse raced. "She's going out Davison Head."

Fred was on his feet now, fearful, uncertain. "I hope—" He barely breathed the words. "I hope she remembers about Channel Rock."

The rock, hidden at high tide, had deceived a number of cruisers, destroyed their props and hulls. Covered by water and darkness, the treacherous reef waited to claim another. "She'll veer off, take the starboard side," Scott said, praying he was right.

The Bayliner gave no ground.

"She knows we're on her trail. She's running without lights."

Did she know, or was she in too much of a hurry to keep an appointment with the two who'd been the legmen for this poisonous operation from the beginning? Was she planning on turning Erin over to those two, let them do her dirty work as they had with the treasury agent and Owen? It had been easy, Scott imagined, for her to kill Toni, whom she'd hated, and not too difficult to kill poor Marilyn in her drunken state. But Erin— Erin would be another matter.

"My God," Fred cried out, "she's going right over it."

She went at full throttle. There is nothing so sickening as the sound of wood scraping against rock, of a ship's hull being crushed by a solid mass of stone, unless it is the sound of plastic ripping under the cutting blades of a reef, pulverizing and punching apart. The engine faltered, and a woman screamed. Davey edged closer to the dark shadows of the unlit boat. Scott threw off his shoes and poised on the bow, straining to see. Davey switched on the big pole lights, and the bright flash lit up the water, swept the sea around them, and finally fell on the small boat that lay tipped on its side, water flooding into the hole in its hull. Beside it a form fought to stay afloat.

Georgie tossed the lifeline. For one chilling moment they watched while it sailed over the waves and landed short of its mark, bounced back in the rolling seas.

Fred hit the water first. He dove into a rising wave. Fred, who'd captained the swim team in college. Taking strong arm-over-arm strokes, he reached the Bayliner just ahead of Scott. One person hung on to the prop; one woman choked for breath, looking done in from the effort. She clutched the long shank of steel. Fred got his arm around her, pulled her free, and the Bayliner lurched a notch closer to capsizing.

Scott reached Fred's side, afraid to see who'd been spared, but hoping. Fred turned, one arm holding his survivor. The floods from the *Mollie O* shone on the pale face. It was Erin, confused but conscious. Scott let out a prayerful sigh of thanks. Fred released his limp charge into Scott's waiting arms and then turned wordlessly, drew a deep breath, and dropped into a wall of whitecapped surf in search of Lorene.

Scott pulled Erin close, held her against his chest as the swell lifted them up and dropped them back down. He held her while they both choked on mouthfuls of salt water, blinded by the frothy spray that blew into their faces from the gusting winds. He'd been so overjoyed to find her alive that he'd ignored the problem of getting her back safely in these seas. Water smashed against them with the force of dinghies colliding, filled up their clothes, weighing them down, sucking them under. Erin offered no resistance. *Have to hold on,* Scott told himself.

On the *Mollie O*, Georgie and Davey were both throwing lines. The ring bobbled in front of Scott and danced out of reach. Waves piled up. New fears came over him as he held Erin with one arm and paddled with the other, kicking desperately to keep their heads above water, only half succeeding. A big roller fell over them, filled the space between them. Erin started to slip. Scott got his hand on her waist, pulled her in. She didn't move. His heart stopped. Then he felt her breast rise. She was alive, but barely. He had to get her on board the *Mollie O*, get her warm, for hypothermia came swiftly in these waters. He worked his way toward the *Mollie O*. It was pitch-dark, and the pleasure boats were too far away to be of any use, but Davey had moved the *Mollie O* closer and waited with lines, shouting encouragement.

It wasn't an easy maneuver, trying to lift someone up over the slippery sides of a boat from the water, with waves pounding on all sides. Scott tried to grab the line, but with Erin in his arms it was impossible. Georgie leaned over and, half hanging by his toes, tried to reach her, with no success. Davey joined in the effort and failed. Scott's legs were like two gas tanks, full and too heavy to lift. He kicked. Nothing happened. He kicked again, and his chest sent stabbing pains to his limbs. He tried once more, and slowly, painfully, boosted her up. Georgie was waiting, and this time caught hold. "Got her," he said, and Scott knew Erin was safe.

Georgie and Davey pulled her up over the side and encased her in blankets. From below, both arms free, Scott treaded water and began to shed clothes. He stripped down to his shorts and felt a welcome freedom of movement and the bite of ice-cold water on his bare legs and arms.

"Come on, Doc," Davey shouted, dangling the line over the side for Scott to grab hold.

Scott waved him off. "Have to help Fred." Erin's cry of protest whimpered in the wind. Slowly, Scott started back to the sinking Bayliner.

The pants and jacket had acted like an anchor. Now at least he had only to fight the thrashing action of the seas. It was enough. Davey worked the wheel, and backed the *Mollie O* within a few feet of the reef. The trouble was holding her there. With the action of the waves and the tide, the boat tended to bounce shoreward. It was only a short swim to the Bayliner, maybe no more than thirty feet. In the water, it looked like a mile. Scott plunged ahead. He went down with a roller, trying not to fight, working to make headway. Another roll. He drifted back to where he started.

Finally, he resorted to a breaststroke that succeeded in getting him through the waves. By the time he reached the reef, the Bayliner listed badly to starboard, and there was no sign of either Fred or Lorene. The cold hadn't bothered him that much before. Maybe the jacket had held in his body heat. Now he began to shiver. He yelled Fred's name. A useless effort. He paid for it with a mouthful of salt water.

Scott managed to reach the Bayliner. He took a deep breath and got under her sinking side. He saw only murky water and the shadow of the cabin hanging dangerously over his head. Davey must have seen the problem. From the boat, the big strobe lights started dancing over the Bayliner, swinging back and forth, lighting up one section and then another. Scott rose to the surface and treaded water, waiting. Finally, the roving spots from Davey's bow picker picked up movement. It was only a splash. Scott started toward it. Fred burst out of a wave, opened his mouth, sucked in air, and went down again. There was total desperation in the act. Scott tucked his knees to his chin and dove after him, down where even Davey's floods couldn't penetrate the darkness—underneath the Bayliner.

Scott used his fingers to feel his way along the broken hull, ran them blindly along the slippery wood, over barnacles, grass, more barnacles, hand over hand. Then he felt something unlike any of the properties of the boat or the sea. He touched hair, bumped shoulders. Arms moved. It was Fred, pulling and tugging desperately against the cruiser's ridgepole. Lorene was trapped under her boat. She'd been down a long time—too long—and Fred couldn't budge her loose. If he continued to try, they would both drown.

With hand signals to Fred, Scott laid his shoulder to the hull. Fred did the same, and they both pushed. Nothing moved. They tried again. Still nothing. Lorene was caught between the reef and the splintered hull, and there was no way two men could dislodge the ten tons of water and hull that held her captive.

Fred wasn't going to give up. Scott's chest constricted like a tied-off blood vessel; his lungs were near bursting. He had to have air. In one push he shot up, broke the surface, and choked for breath, throat and chest burning. A second later, Fred followed, took another deep gasping breath, and prepared to go down again. Fred was weakening, his breath coming in uneven jerks. In that dangerous condition he would have gone. He would have gone and maybe drowned, but forces beyond his control made further attempts irrelevant. A large wave struck, and the Bayliner rolled off the rock and sank. While Scott and Fred watched, Lorene's lifeless body floated to the surface.

Twenty-Three

There was nothing they could do for Lorene. Scott kneeled on the wet deck, his bare knees digging painfully into the slippery wood as he tried mouth-to-mouth resuscitation, more to satisfy Fred than out of hope he could breathe life back into Lorene's flaccid body. She'd been lost minutes ago, died, he guessed, when she'd struck her head on the bottom of her boat.

"I'm sorry, Fred," Scott said.

Fred stared blankly at the slender white fingers protruding from under the piece of tarp they draped over her and said nothing.

Vic and Billy arrived and rafted alongside. Vic cracked out some blankets from his cabin and handed one to Scott. Scott hadn't even thought about the cold or how ridiculous he looked in his shorts and the wet sports shirt that clung to him like plastic wrap. Vic looked at Fred, still standing over Lorene, getting rained on and dripping water, and stuck one of the blankets in his hands. "Better put this over you."

Fred didn't move. Scott unfolded the blanket and threw it around Fred's shoulders, and they left him to his lonely vigil.

Scott found Erin hiding under the tentlike protection of a Poncho. She was on the bow of the *Nellie J*, leaning against the rail, staring into water. When she turned her face to look up at him, her eyes filled with tears. "I couldn't stop her, Scott. I didn't know what to do. I—I just jumped."

"A good thing you did."

Underneath all the rain gear she wore an old pair of

Georgie's sweats. She looked so small and defenseless. He kissed her, a long dizzying kiss, and the blanket slipped to the deck. The wind whipped at his bare legs, and he started to shiver.

Erin stood back and considered his condition with a concerned frown. "Scott, you're going to freeze to death."

He gathered the blanket up and wrapped himself in it again. "I'm—I'm fine." The shivers turned violent, and he began to shake all over.

Georgie walked over, curious. "I've seen scuba divers do that, shake for hours that way. It's going in without a wet suit. Kills them every time."

Billy took one look at Scott, climbed across to his own ship, and returned a minute later holding a pile of clothes. "Get out of those wet things before you make me dizzy."

"Better get some for Fred," Scott stuttered, accepting the clothes gratefully.

Changed into Billy's jeans and Vic's old fish-net sweater, Scott was a long way from warm, but the shakes stopped. Feeling better, he sought Fred. His friend was still on the bow of the *Mollie O*, standing over Lorene, the blanket resting loosely on his shoulders. He still held the clothes Billy had brought, but had made no attempt to do anything with them.

"Getting pneumonia won't help anything."

Fred looked up and slowly began to peel off his pants and shorts. Suddenly he found his voice. "You knew . . . about Toni?"

"Yes." No point in telling him he'd only known for a few hours.

Fred pulled on the dry trousers. They were too long, but Fred didn't notice. "Sorry, Scottie. Don't know how it started. Never meant to go so far."

"It's in the past, Fred." So much in the past there seemed little to forgive.

"My—my fault." Fred slipped on a shirt and began rolling up the pants legs. "Poor Lorene, we—we should've had children. Would've helped. She wanted to. It was me that didn't." His lips trembled, and as if the memory were too much, stopped talking.

Scott guessed he was going back in time, thinking of those twists in his wife's behavior pattern, warnings he'd chosen to ignore, just as he'd always avoided anything unpleasant. Scott imagined he was asking himself what he might have done to stop a lonely and desperate woman from taking a wrong turn, a turn none of them had seen. Perhaps, sadly, one no one could have prevented. *In an obtuse way, I'm as much to blame as Fred. I'm the one who drove Toni into another man's arms, robbed Lorene of all she treasured in the world.*

Fred sat down on the deck and looked up at Scott through red eyes. "I loved her, and I failed her."

Scott placed a reassuring hand on his friend's shoulder. "Go below and get warm, Fred."

Vic walked over carrying rain slickers, a bottle of brandy, and some water glasses. He poured a generous portion of brandy into one and stuck it in Fred's hand. Fred took it, sipped once, and started to cry.

Erin was in the *Nellie J*'s galley digging around for coffee when Scott found her again. "About Brice," she said. "You knew he lied about the artifacts?"

"Yes," Scott said.

Unhappiness filled her face. "I wanted to find out. That's why I went over there. It seemed so odd—the fake in Victoria, that the others would be authentic. I'm not the expert Brice is, but I could tell when I looked. The work was crude, very unlike the one Mrs. McDonald showed us in Victoria." She set the coffeepot under the water tap and filled it. "What do you think it means about Brice?"

"I imagine he purchased some of Owen's pieces and knew Owen was replacing them with fakes."

"You think he lied because he feared he'd be dragged in?"

"It could be something like that."

"To cover up. A man like him!" She shook her head in bewilderment. "Will it have to come out? It could damage his reputation very badly."

"Depends. If it was an innocent purchase, an honest mis-

186

take, maybe not. But if he was helping Owen launder drug money, they'll throw the book at him."

She nodded understanding and went back to the stove and the coffee.

Fifteen minutes passed while they waited in the cold, the wind blowing the rain in a soft spray across the decks. This nightmare wasn't over yet, and with Leroy's delay, the tension grew.

Vic looked off across the bay. "Leroy said the bust would be 'round here somewhere. What you think, Doc?"

"Battleship Island is my guess. Gives them a clear shot into Canada if anything goes wrong. What bothers me, Lorene was racing here to warn them."

"You're thinking they should be here by now."

"Where they going with it?" Davey wondered.

"Transfer to fast boats, more drops, maybe to the fishermen."

"They been transferring coke and hash off Iceberg for months," Vic said.

Scott looked sharply at his friend. "How do you know that?"

"Me and Billy put it together. Some of the boats"—Vic and Billy exchanged amused glances—"not just the Indians, been coming up with big profits."

Davey agreed. "Anyone who says he's making a killing this season is a liar. Not on fish, he's not."

"A liar or a drug pusher," Billy added bitterly. "The kids've been getting it from somewhere."

"I don't think they'll be going to Iceberg tonight. Not after Marilyn blew the whistle on it," Scott said.

"Hey, Doc, is that why they knocked her off?" Georgie asked.

Scott thought of the look on Lorene's face when Fred danced with Marilyn. Had Marilyn's tendency to talk too much been the reason? "It played a part." He hadn't told any of them about Lorene and the killings, only about her role in the drug operation. He imagined they guessed the rest and, thinking of

Fred, still sitting alone on the *Mollie O* refusing all efforts at communication, saw no useful purpose in discussing it. Scott was grateful.

Erin came on deck to refill the coffee cups and told Scott she'd managed to reach Al on the radio. Georgie, standing by the reel, said he thought he saw the sheriff's patrol boat coming through Davison. Erin went to find Fred.

Leroy stepped off his Whaler onto the *Nellie J*. He accepted the story of Lorene with a fatalistic lift of his shoulders and quickly moved to the problem at hand. The key members of the drug-smuggling ring were yet to be rounded up, and catching them with the goods, a vital part of shutting them down, would not be easy. They looked anxiously at each other.

"You and Harold aren't going alone on this deal, are you, Sheriff?"

Leroy wore his usual noncommittal face. "Treasury boys are coming in by chopper any minute now. More of my men are driving from Friday. Won't be long."

"What about the drug runners?" Georgie asked.

"Word is they left Friday Harbor fifteen minutes ago."

Scott looked at his watch. "They should be rounding Davison Head in ten minutes."

"That's the way I figure it," Leroy said.

Vic, who'd come out of Korea with a Silver Star and two oak-leaf clusters, laughed. "C'mon, Sheriff, loosen up. You and Harold can't go alone, and you can't wait, and we're here."

They all wanted to go, each for his own reason. For Scott, to expiate guilt; for the others, maybe it answered their frustrations or maybe it was to pay back those from among their own who'd violated a trust. Vic pointed out that the sheriff's patrol boat would be spotted right away, but that the skiff, lightweight aluminum and sturdy, would be less suspicious, less likely to alert the drug runners. Vic scored with this point. Leroy inspected the darkened skies. "Wonder where the hell they got to?"

Off Davison Head a light flickered from a small boat heading west, toward Battleship Island. They watched Leroy anxiously for his answer. Leroy gave in, exacting the promise that they'd all back off as soon as the treasury officers arrived. Scott, Billy, and Davey would go with Vic and Leroy in Vic's skiff, get just close enough to spot them, and alert the chopper. Harold would follow in the Whaler, lead the chopper in. Georgie, Fred, and the rest of the crews would stay aboard the boats with Erin, and alert the deputies when they arrived. Georgie didn't like it.

"Stop bitching," Vic said as his men lowered the skiff. "Too many would slow us down."

"What about him?" Georgie pointed to Fred, who'd come onto the *Nellie J* and was just waking up to what was going on.

"I'm going," Fred said, setting his lips grimly.

Scott was going to argue that Fred was in too highly an emotional state, that he might not act rationally, and a lot of other reasons that boiled down to the same thing. But one look at Fred's face, and he knew none of it would be of any use. Vic shrugged. "Let's get going."

Vic threw the throttle forward, and the skiff exploded on the sea. Scott looked back at Erin, who was huddled next to Georgie, and grinned at her. But Erin wasn't smiling.

"We'll head him off going around McCracken Point," Vic said.

Leroy nodded. His hand rested on the big Colt .38 strapped to his side. Scott didn't know much about how the drug-smuggling operation worked, but he had an idea. In this case, two small boats meeting in the dark of night, one to make the drop, the other to pick up the goods and beat it to the next transfer point, on land or to another boat. Scott imagined the one running the university craft was a student, someone recruited by Lorene, maybe when she'd worked on one of her community projects, like the University Dropout Rehabilitation Center. But who was piloting the receiving craft? A onetime hireling with a fast boat, or a regular? Or, the thought flashed in his mind, someone who knew more about the operation than that, who'd been in it all along. Scott's arm and leg muscles tensed up in anticipation.

The wind and rain eased, and the big diesel put out a

thundering rumble as the skiff closed in on Henry Island. Leroy didn't like it.

"What's the matter?"

"With that wind dying, they might hear our engine."

"And they'll see a boatload of drunk fishermen joyriding."

Leroy wasn't reassured.

"Want I should slow down?"

"Can't chance that either. I guess our best hope is surprise."

Vic nodded and threw the throttle wide open. The skiff wasn't meant for speed or crowds. She was a working boat—no soft spots, just bare metal and a seat for the helmsman. They bounced around in its big metal insides, each bounce cutting into legs and elbows, jarring insides. Bruised and sore, Scott struggled to his knees and got a hold on the gunwales as Vic ran mercilessly on through the passage between Pearl and Henry. No one complained.

From the opening he cut around the point and struck a course south and west. Battleship Island, named for its resemblance to a battleship when viewed from the strait, was an undeveloped state park with a small beach at low tide and a rocky headland on its south side. Vic aimed for the south, hoping to take cover behind the headland and approach the drug runners from their blind side. It wasn't a bad plan, and Vic did a good job maneuvering around the rocks. He tucked her up against a reef on the lee side of Battleship just as the university boat poked its nose out of Speiden.

"We'll wait here until he clears Barren Island," Vic said.

Leroy nodded and looked anxiously into the empty sky. Still no sign of the chopper, and Scott knew what Leroy was thinking. Would they arrive in time for the transfer, and, if not, could a skiffload of amateurs handle the situation? Dare they move in against men who quite likely had guns and were sure to be desperate enough to try anything?

The university boat, small and speedy, reached the island and began flashing its lights across the open water. The answering flash came from behind Bell Rock and put a beacon of light up the slot like the floods from an ocean liner.

"He doesn't see us," Davey said, a nervous tremor in his voice.

Vic took the skiff around the reef, and they caught a full view of the small runabout hanging alongside a seaplane, a plane just like the one off Campbell River. The possible became the probable—Charlie and Jerry. Vic's hand hovered on the throttle, and Scott began counting off seconds.

Leroy looked fretfully at the sky. Whatever else they were, these drug smugglers weren't amateurs. If given too much time they'd make their transfer and be on their way. The plane, of course, could take off, be out of range in seconds. Another problem also presented itself. If the skiff reached them before they could take off, they would surely dump the evidence, and without the proof Leroy and the treasury people wouldn't have a case. Without backup from the sky, it was risky to go ahead, but if they didn't move they risked losing everything. They watched and waited.

A wave splashed over the bow and hosed them down. Leroy gave the signal. Vic gunned it. They vaulted out from the rocks like an overfed whale. It was a sloppy operation from beginning to end, but the thundering rumble of the wind drowned the noise of the diesel, allowed them time to spring their surprise. Vic nearly ran the small plane down with the skiff, slammed against a pontoon, and quickly threw a line around the struts, rendering the plane helpless. A good deal of scurrying and swearing followed. The student on the runabout panicked and jumped overboard, floundering in the waves. Davey fished him out. He was a frightened boy of nineteen or twenty. Leroy put a warning shot over the nose of the plane. Panic spread.

"This is the law. Come out with your arms raised."

Bullets zinged off the metal sides of the skiff.

"Jee-sus," Davey murmured.

A distant rumble shook the skies, and the chopper moved down on them. Harold pulled up in the patrol boat, and the plane door flew open and one of its occupants pitched a silver object into the water. The splash was followed by another. The guns! Scott feared what would go next. Overhead, the deafening clatter of the chopper made its presence felt in a terrifying way. The pilot burst out of the plane, hands raised, and surrendered himself into Leroy's hands. His companion, the short, stocky one, the one called Charlie, hesitated at the door, holding something.

"Hey," Billy shouted, "he's going to dump the stuff."

Fred, who'd maintained a robotlike presence during the run, suddenly came alive. He leaped onto the pontoon, shot up the strut, and dove through the plane's open door like the entire line of the Chicago Bears. Charlie went down, the stuff still in his hands. Fearful for Fred, Scott followed through the cabin door. Fred had Charlie pinned between the cockpit seat and the instrument panel and was pounding on him as he might attack a punching bag. It was a different Fred—eyes glazed over, jaw set—who beat on Charlie with a merciless barrage of lefts and rights, hard chops that made meat of Charlie's face, pounded the wind out of his lungs. All the rage and frustration of Fred's nightmare erupted in those blows. It wasn't much of a struggle from Charlie's point of view. He held his hands in front of his face, trying to protect himself against angry fists that found their mark anyway, and blood started flowing all over the place. Fred kept it up, not stopping, for if he had, he would have seen that Charlie was already a lump of raw flesh with not an ounce of fight left in him. Scott pulled on Fred's arms and dragged him to the open door. Fred was breathing hard and still had fire in his eyes.

"He's had enough, Fred."

Fred stared dumbly at the thoroughly beaten Charlie and nodded, and he and Scott pulled Charlie and the bag of cocaine to the door and into Leroy's waiting hands. Leroy took one look at Charlie's puffed-up face and swore as Fred stumbled back onto the skiff, drooping badly. He'd expended every last ounce of energy in the attack on Charlie. Leroy loaded them all up into the Whaler—the pilot, Charlie, and the student. Only Scott knew there was still one left.

Scott climbed into the plane. The slender, bone-tough gunman, the one called Jerry, backed up behind the luggage racks, his hands in front of his face, his knees tucked under his chin. Scott took a step toward him.

"Get away from me!"

The toughness was gone from the voice. Fred's brutal assault on his partner had removed any thought of resistance. It had also tempered Scott's own desire for revenge. Something else, however, began to tick off in Scott's head, an idea that had begun when he'd seen it was the same two from the *Pilgrim*. These two weren't ordinary lackeys. They'd killed the treasury man and quite possibly Owen as well, probably pumped shot into Marilyn's dead body to cover up for Lorene's own work.

Now, the one with all the mouth on the beach that night cowered under the racks. In his present state, scared out of his wits, he presented an opportunity. If properly enticed, he might tell what he knew about the drug ring that had spread its network through the islands. Lorene wasn't the only one. There had to be someone else—a lieutenant maybe, even a general. Leroy was busy on the Whaler. There was no one standing over them to see. No one to stop Scott as he wrapped his fingers around Jerry's neck and held him to the floor.

"You're choking me," Jerry whimpered. "Let me go. I know my rights."

"You killed three people. That takes away all rights."

"I didn't . . . wasn't me. I didn't kill the T-man. Charlie . . . Charlie did it."

"And Owen?"

"The bitch—she told us to do it. It was the bitch."

"I'm not interested in her. I want to know about the other one. I want a name. Who were you taking this stuff to? Who's the one you answer to besides Lorene Chapman?"

Jerry's face screwed up. "Don't know what you're talking about."

Scott's fingers tightened around Jerry's neck, squeezed the cords until Jerry's eyes started to bulge. "I can shut off the carotid artery this way. You'll be dead in an instant, and no one will ever know it wasn't an accident."

"Uk, " Jerry croaked.

Scott pressed harder. Jerry tried to yell, but couldn't. How far dared he go with it? Scott wondered. Where was the point of no return? Scott thought of Toni and Marilyn and Billie's kids and Prissie. He squeezed another notch. Jerry made a sound. No words came out. Scott let go. Jerry choked wildly, fighting for air. "Who?" Scott said fiercely, pressing on the vocal chords again. "Give me a name."

"Ran . . . Randall," Jerry gasped, spitting up bile. "Brice Ran . . . dall."

Twenty-Four

Scott felt a deep ache as Fred piled into the chopper with Lorene for her last trip to the mainland. There was no way to help, nothing to be done. Only time could help his friend.

The light still burned in Al's window when they drove up in Leroy's wagon. Out on the pass the waters were settling down. A piece of moon found its way out of the black layers of cloud and cast a golden glow over Goose Island. Erin called out a soft "Good night" to Leroy as she and Scott slipped out of the patrol car. Leroy waved the one-arm salute and rolled quietly back onto the road, headed toward town and, Scott hoped, a well-earned night's sleep without the television cameramen and the rest of the Seattle media that had poured onto the island by plane and chopper to record the now famed drug bust.

They woke Al from a sound sleep in his chair, but he was far too anxious to learn what had happened to be annoyed. The questions tumbled one after another without pause. It had gone smoothly enough, Scott told Al. Leroy had turned Charlie and Jerry over to the treasury boys along with Bob Delaney, who was already indicating a willingness to testify as a material witness to the drug-laundering business, which he'd been in up to his neck.

Al wasn't surprised about Brice. "I read not long ago he was having trouble with one of his buildings that couldn't pass code. He was being sued all over the place. Catches up with them. What I don't understand is Lorene. She came from a wealthy family. Why would she mess around with the drug business?"

Scott replied. "From what Cynthia told me, her parents lost

most of their money, and Lorene had this obsession that Fred only hung around because of her inheritance."

"You mean Fred didn't know she was broke? He thought all the money she was raking in from the drug operation came from her trust?"

"That's it."

"But I thought Fred did pretty well in commodities."

"I think he does, but he's up and down, a natural-born gambler. Some people love living on the edge. Fred is one of those."

Al frowned at Erin. "Which reminds me, why the blue blazes did you go with Lorene on that boat?"

"It seems stupid now, but it started out innocently enough. She asked me to drive her over to the boat, said she had to retrieve a coffeepot and that we could have a chance to chat." Erin's cheeks pinked in the firelight. "We'd been having a pleasant conversation."

"You told her about the masks?"

"A good deal more than that, I'm afraid. I never in the world guessed. She was a friend of yours, and I assumed—"

"There's no way you could have known."

"Anyway, I could see she wanted company, and there was something so lonely about her. Then when we reached the boat she started undoing the lines, and before I knew it, we were on our way. I didn't get really alarmed until I saw she was actually going out in the storm, and after we were under way she started saying wild things, accusing me of coming on to Fred, and . . ." Erin shook her head, remembering. "I knew then she was quite crazy. I had the weirdest idea she thought I was someone else."

"I'm sure she did," Scott said.

Puzzled, Erin started to say something. Al interrupted. "How did those hired gunmen happen to operate a ship carrying university students?"

Scott explained about Preston Fields and how he'd fallen into the mess.

"Poor Pres," Erin said.

"Poor Pres, my eye!" Al delivered a stern lecture on faculty ethics, and stopped finally when he thought of another question. "What about the necklace and the masks? What was that all about?"

"The masks are simple. Owen and Randall bought and sold the artifacts to launder the drug money. It's a pretty good way to drop a lot of cash unnoticed, and the value of art fluctuates just like diamonds or gold or land. They buy a collection of African art at auction for cash and then when they sell it again it's clean. Same thing with the land, running it through Canada with dummy companies. They probably had a number of such maneuvers with fishing boats, oil leases, who knows what all."

"Why the fakes?"

"Owen wanted to conceal what they were doing."

Al was still puzzled. "I can see why Lorene was afraid Erin would ruin everything, but why did she kill Owen?"

"You know Owen. He was the kind who couldn't pass up an extra buck, and he knew something no one else knew, that it was Lorene who'd put drugs into Toni's drink the night of Randall's party celebrating the opening of the Center Mall. There I'm a little unsure, but my guess is Lorene drove Toni to the ferry landing, put the Mercedes in gear, and —"

Erin drew in her breath. "Oh, no! She was jealous of Toni, too."

"But why did they break into your place?" Al asked.

"Lorene put them up to that, too. They were after Toni's appointment book, which undoubtedly had Toni's notation about meeting Lorene. Or Lorene was afraid it did, and she feared sooner or later someone would see and figure it out." Scott didn't tell them about Toni and Fred or that Owen had found out about their affair. "Lorene imagined all kinds of things in the last year."

"Mmm," Al said, but nothing more.

Erin had another concern. "Was Brice Randall involved in the murders?"

"I doubt it. My guess is that when Brice received that call from Leroy about the masks, he panicked, told Leroy they were valuable when he knew they were fakes. I think he hoped to switch his collection back and cover up the lie, not very smart for a smart operator like him."

"What about the people who own the *Pilgrim*?"

"Camstar? Their dummy company. It may have connections with some international drug money as well. I tried to track it down, but found only the subsidiary they used in their land deals, which makes me think they're tied up in foreign trusts. I imagine our treasury men will have to unravel it. All I know for a fact is that Owen was an officer, a front man. Brice and Lorene were too smart for that."

Al's eyelids began to droop. "You still haven't explained about the necklace."

"Or how the mask turned up in Victoria."

"I suppose Jerry and Charlie were doing a little freelancing."

"I guess that's the size of it, all right." Al yawned again.

Scott rose from his chair. "I'll leave you now and let you both get some sleep."

"See you tomorrow," Al mumbled sleepily, shuffling off to the bedroom.

Erin trapped Scott at the door. "You're not telling all you know," she accused with a smile.

She was standing close, and the sweet scent of her perfume wafted between them. He kissed her, a long lingering kiss, held her tight until he felt her lips tremble and she was kissing him back. When he let her go there was no confusion in her eyes. She knew as well as he that it had not been a brotherly kiss, and that whatever direction this would take them, they were no longer just friends. "Good night," he whispered.

As he walked home it all came as clear as the moon lighting the path in front of him. He would go back to his surgical practice. Ralph had known all along that he'd need time to sort things out, but that he'd come back to what he knew best. He suspected Erin had known that, too. He wasn't sure how long he'd be able to tolerate it—the rules, the forms, the screeners poring over his records, telling him how to treat his patients—but he knew Erin would understand that, too, that it would always be that way between them—understanding, everything shared, all the things that had been missing between him and Toni. Scott looked across the rippling seas in front of his house and felt an inner peace he hadn't known in a long time.

Scott was pouring himself a bowl of breakfast cereal when Dandy announced an early-morning visitor. Somehow Scott wasn't surprised to see Vic standing on the doorstep, looking unhappy. "C'mon in, Vic. Good show last night."

"Yeah," Vic said, but there was no cheer in his voice or his eyes.

"Coffee?"

"Can't stay." Vic said, not moving out of the doorway.

"Come in, at least, and tell me what's bugging you."

Shrugging, Vic walked in, followed Scott into the kitchen, settled himself on a stool, and watched while Scott proceeded to fill up the coffeepot. "Don't know how to tell you this," he said.

"Then don't."

"Nope. Time to square things."

"If you don't think last night did that—"

"You don't know what I got to tell you. You don't know what a damn fool thing I did."

Scott plugged in the coffeepot and turned to look into his friend's worried face. "You mean like taking the mask and the necklace from Owen's house and trying to peddle it in Victoria? Is that the damn fool thing you're referring to?"

Vic's mouth gaped. "How the hell did you know that?"

"You went there the night of the murder."

Vic nodded dumbly. "I wanted to have it out with Owen. He lost me a pile on the fish-buyer deal, and I was going to wring it out of him. Trouble was, he was dead when I got there."

"And you didn't call the sheriff?"

"I was going to, and then I got to thinking how it might look, me with such damn good reason to want the son of a bitch dead. I started to go, and it suddenly hit me that that bastard screwed me out of two hundred thousand bucks, and now I'd never get it back."

"So you took the mask and the necklace? You could've taken a lot more."

"All I wanted was some of what Owen cost me." He shook his head morosely. "But the mask turned out to be as phony as Owen."

"What about the necklace?"

"That's why I came." Vic reached into his jacket pocket and pulled out a long gold chain and handed it to Scott.

The links of elephant hair and gold fell into a heavy snakelike coil in Scott's hand. Scott examined the interlocking twists of bright gold, but he already knew from its weight that it was the one authentic piece in Owen's collection. "I have to tell you, Vic. This piece *is* worth something."

Vic shook his head in disgust. "I don't give a shit. It's not worth the gut ache it's cost me, I can tell you that. All I want to know is, what do I do with it now?"

Scott studied his friend's unhappy face. Vic had paid a dear price for his indiscretion. Some would say he'd paid a greater price than was due. "Mmm," Scott said. "Do you trust me?"

"What kind of dumb question is that?"

"I mean, do you trust this to me?"

"I was a damn fool—you know that, Doc—but I don't see myself going up on murder charges for lifting a pile of African junk. Don't much like the idea of landing in the slammer either. But those are the horrors of war, I suppose." He shook his head and looked glum again.

"You may not have to if you leave it to me and keep your mouth shut."

Vic left like a man with a giant burden removed.

In the sheriff's office, Leroy laid the necklace in front of him on his desk and studied it. "You trying to tell me you found this thing on one of those two clowns last night and you're just returning it now?"

"That's right," Scott said, staring back into the sheriff's doubting eyes. "Everything was happening so fast I forgot about it."

Leroy leaned back in the swivel chair and contemplated the ceiling. "Okay," he said finally. "I'll buy it. Now you can deliver a message for me. Tell your friends thanks. I couldn't have done it last night without them."

"Vic and the boys will be pleased to hear that."

Leroy's lips played one of those half-smiles. "Yes, it was Vic I was thinking about."